The Tower of Air

BOOK THREE

JIMMY FINCHER SAGA

The Tower of Air

JAMES DASHNER

ILLUSTRATED BY MICHAEL PHIPPS

SWEETWATER BOOKS
AN IMPRINT OF CEDAR FORT, INC.
SPRINGVILLE, UTAH

No part of this book may be reproduced in any form whatsoever, whether by graphic, visual, electronic, film, microfilm, tape recording, or any other means, without prior written permission of the publisher, except in the case of brief passages embodied in critical reviews and articles.

This is a work of fiction. The characters, names, incidents, places, and dialogue are products of the author's imagination and are not to be construed as real. The views expressed within this work are the sole responsibility of the author and do not necessarily reflect the position of Cedar Fort, Inc., or any other entity.

ISBN 13: 978-1-55517-801-7

Published by Sweetwater Books, an imprint of Cedar Fort, Inc.
2373 W. 700 S., Springville, UT 84663
Distributed by Cedar Fort, Inc., www.cedarfort.com

LIBRARY OF CONGRESS CONTROL NUMBER: 2004108699

Cover design by Rebecca Jensen
Cover design © 2012 by Lyle Mortimer

Printed in the United States of America

10 9 8 7 6 5 4 3 2 1

Printed on acid-free paper

*This one is for Dad, up in heaven.
A lot of the material and ideas in this
saga come from my imagination. Jimmy's
love for his dad is not one of them.*

Acknowledgments

A big thanks to the people who helped me with the third book, especially my talented wife, Lynette, as well as Matt and Tristi Pinkston, the insane Bahlmann family (Shirley, Zack, Brian, and Michael), and Nikki Shaffer, Natalie Roach, and Nicole Cunningham at Cedar Fort. I'm also thankful to Georgia Carpenter, Vachelle Johnson, and Angie Harris for their hard work at promoting the series.

A huge thanks to Bryce Mortimer for his talent and efforts at recording the audio versions. He's now making a much bigger and more praiseworthy sacrifice than sitting in a recording studio.

I am grateful to Dave Wolverton, Tracy Hickman, Laura Hickman, and L. E. Modesitt Jr. for taking time out of their extremely busy schedules to help out and advise dreamers like myself.

Of course, the biggest thanks goes to you, the one holding this book. Without the readers, Jimmy Fincher wouldn't have made it this far.

Contents

Prologue

In the midst of a world that was gray and wet, the creature stirred, and the sound of metallic clatter was dulled by wind and rain.

The creature was hunting.

Its black wings still shifted occasionally between the solid firmness of what they were becoming, and the wavering mix of shadow and nightmare they had once been. The entity felt stronger now, with a renewed sense of certain accomplishment. As the evolution quickened, so did its hope. Success— the *preparation*—was at hand.

The rain intensified, pelting the creature from all sides as the wind tore haphazardly from every direction. The heavy chain hanging around its neck was beginning to hurt, but the thought of what lay ahead enlivened and encouraged the winged beast. It would be worth it, the pain of carrying the chain in this long and arduous flight. Well, the chains. The flying abomination was not alone.

If the storm were to abate, the sounds of flapping wings and rattling chains would have filled the air with a frightening sense of doom. They were many, and their purpose was one. This was fortunate considering the bad weather.

The creature strained its black eyes to see into the distance, but it was hopeless. There was only gray, and the quick sparkles of thrashing rain. The roar of the wind made communication impossible.

So they flew, and they searched, and they waited for the storm to end its fury.

There, in the distance, something caught the creature's attention.

It was impossible to tell for sure, but it was at least different from the constant blurry visage of the past few hours of the storm. Something dark, far below, moving up and down in a definite pattern, a contrast from the random movement of cloud and rain. Could it be?

The others did not see it yet. After a long intake of breath, the creature let out a piercing scream, putting all of its effort into making the cry louder than the sound of the storm. Most of the others looked, and came closer to find out what was transpiring.

Since speaking was out of the question, the beast merely pointed toward the dark object below. The others nodded.

They began their descent, chains and wings flapping in the wind.

They had finally found me.

There is a place, where a ribbon of black marble cuts through an inky sea of gray waters. The stone-cold path goes on forever in both directions, no one yet ever reaching an end on either side. The monotony, the *sameness*, of the lonely trail is only broken by round landings of stone with stacked iron rings in the middle, gateways to countless worlds. There is no sky; at least, the swirling mists never allow the sight of it.

The Black Curtain, the rift between that world and ours was beginning to rip once again, the Blocking steadily losing its power.

The place of frightful wonder to which the Curtain leads is called The Blackness.

I had been there before.

I would be returning very soon.

I'm Jimmy Fincher, and this is my nightmare.

There is so much that I must do.
I must find the Tower of Three Days,
and understand its secret.
I must seek out the one known as Erifani Tup.
I must solve the riddle of the Red Disk.
Most important of all, I must find the only one
who can save us all.
I must find the Dream Warden.
There is so much that I must do . . .

CHAPTER 1

Lots of Water

The ocean was big and dreary, and I hated it.

We had been floating on top of the dang thing for weeks, endlessly searching for something that perhaps did not exist. Even Joseph grew doubtful, and his cheerful demeanor had waned considerably with every passing day. The clues were as scarce as the ocean was vast. We were looking for a place where it was always *three days at the same time*, somewhere in the ocean. That was pretty much it, all we had to go on.

The Tower of Three Days.

It made no sense to me, and I had never felt so completely useless, without any hope whatsoever. How in the world could you take that one clue, and then go and have a look-see throughout the entire *ocean*? It bordered on insanity to even try.

It was almost evening on the thirty-third day when we had our first breakthrough.

The day was beautiful, cloudless and bright. I woke up that morning feeling better physically than I had in quite some time. The first couple of weeks on the ocean had been absolute misery, with nausea my constant companion, and barfing a regular activity. Tanaka stayed well clear of me after meals. He'd had more than one run-in with the Jimmy Fincher puke brigade, and he told us that if he only accomplished one more thing in life, it would be to avoid being spewed on by me ever again.

Our yacht was extremely luxurious and comfortable, with plenty of food. Our captain told us we could last for months if we had to. The boat was nowhere near full capacity, but had been stocked as if we would have a full load. The mystery of how it had all been paid for was still up in the air. Joseph had either robbed a bank or sweet-talked a rich old Japanese widow into giving her husband's fortune away. He answered most of our questions, but not that one. We didn't need to worry about that, not yet, he had said. We didn't argue, because there were plenty of other things to grill him about.

Joseph's experience after being taken by the Shadow Ka on that scary day when I blocked the Black Curtain was very similar to Rayna's story. He'd been flown for many miles through the shifting mists of the Blackness, until finally he had seen a massive black object looming before him. It was made of the same black gooey substance that Rayna had plunged into when she was younger and had been abducted by a Ka.

A black carving of a face. Hers. Joseph's experience was only different in one respect. The face had been his.

The pack of Ka tore into the eye of that face, and Joseph was suddenly thrown through a terrifying maze of nightmares and visions. Then, just before a slumber from which he would have never awakened, the *girl* had appeared, and saved his life.

The girl who I first saw so many weeks ago, waiting for me under the door in the woods. The Giver who wore jeans and sneakers.

She saved his life, releasing him from the living nightmare of the face.

Her words at that time had chilled Joseph. She said she would die for him, just before he was ripped away, out of the darkness. Very strange. And very creepy.

After the ordeal, Joseph had spent several days with the Givers, learning much about many things. Some he had since shared with us, some he had promised for a future time. I was thinking about all of this on the morning of the thirty-third day, standing in my favorite spot at the highest point of the entire ship, looking out into the endless horizon where the blues of ocean and sky met in a distinct line.

That's when I saw something strange floating in the distance.

It was white and sparkly, bobbing in the waters like the last lonely Cheerio in a Sunday morning breakfast bowl. I watched it float there for a while, wondering what object could end up out here in the middle of nowhere. Perhaps it was a dead fish. I was just about to lose interest and search out everyone else on the boat to see what was in store for the day, when it got close enough that I could see that it was definitely not a dead fish.

It was something straight out of the storybooks.

CHAPTER 2

The Lonely Dead Man

Intrigued, I ran down the stairs and into the main cabin, looking for someone who could help me retrieve the thing from the water. Our captain was standing at the main controls of the ship, methodically getting things ready for another day's journey to nowhere. He glanced at me, said hello, and then went back to his duties.

His name was Drake, but we all took the lead from his crew and called him Captain Tinkles. Now, there's something that just ain't right about calling a man Tinkles, but his crew referred to him by no other name. It had something to do with an old story from back when they were all in the Navy, but they refused to tell us the details. Every time I spoke with him, I cringed if I had to use the name. Usually, I just stuck with "Captain" and left off the disturbing second part.

"Captain," I said, "there's something floating up near the front of the yacht that I think we should try to bring on board."

"Oh yeah?" he replied. His voice was grainy, as if he were mixing cement in his mouth while trying to speak. He nodded his head toward the front window. "What is it, a retired dolphin or something?" He didn't laugh, so I wasn't completely sure it had been a joke.

"Just come look. I don't think you'll be disappointed. Do you have something we could reach down and grab it with?"

"Yeah, boy, if it's worth grabbin'. Come on."

He stepped out of the cabin back into the open, with me right behind him. He grabbed a long pole with a net on the end of it from the supply boxes, and headed for the front part of the ship. Joseph, Rayna, and Miyoko had come out while I was talking to the captain, and they were up front pointing at the same object I had seen.

"Ho, there!" yelled the captain. "What you got your eyes glued on? You telling me this boy ain't lying?"

"Ah, good," said Joseph in his whispery voice, the pale sun glimmering off his bald head. "I was just about to go looking for that." He pointed at the net and pole. "So, Jimmy, I take it you saw this little gem, too, huh?"

"Yeah, I hope it's what I think it is."

"There's no doubt that there's something inside of it," Rayna said. She was a member of The Alliance, a mysterious group of people that had dedicated their lives to helping the Givers prepare for the inevitable battle against the Shadow Ka and the Stompers. Her disfigured face and strange green clothes no longer fazed me.

Captain Tinkles leaned out over the railing and reached toward the water with his pole. Our ship was huge, so he had to really stretch himself and extend the pole as far as he possibly could. After several failed attempts, one of which just about sent him swimming, he grabbed the shiny object with a final burst of effort and a heavy grunt.

"Aha! Got the little—"

"Watch your language, there, Tinkle-Boy," said Joseph, cutting him off.

Tinkles pulled the long pole up, hand over hand, and then laid it on the deck of the boat. We all stared at the object, with a sense of reverent awe.

Dad came up from behind.

"What's everyone gawking at?" he asked.

When he saw the source of our wonder, he stopped short.

"What the—" He bent down and picked it up.

In one of those moments where you just can't help but state the obvious, Dad announced to everyone what we had just discovered.

"It's a bottle."

He paused.

"With a note in it."

❧⁂☙

Dad knelt down and we all crowded around him as he fumbled with the bottle.

It was green glass, the shape of an old-fashioned Coke bottle. Despite having floated in the largest washtub in the world for who knows how long, it was covered in spots with slimy dirt and grime. But the glass was just clean enough to see the rolled piece of paper inside, a magical note waiting to be read. A message in a bottle. It was something that everyone had dreamed about at one time in his or her life. I never knew which would be cooler, sending a message and having someone find it, or finding one sent by someone else.

We were all anxious, and urged Dad to hurry and open it.

He grabbed the twist-off lid, squeezed and turned. At first it didn't budge, but Dad strained until veins were popping out of his neck, and it soon gave way. He twisted the lid until it came off, and handed it to me.

He turned the bottle over, and shook it. The note was stubborn, and kept getting stuck on the lip of the bottle, not wanting to come out. Dad finally had to have Miyoko stick her little pinky finger in the bottle and slowly drag the piece of paper out. She handed it back to Dad.

He bent over and placed the note on the deck and unrolled the paper, spreading it out with his hands. He then read its message out loud, although we could all see it for ourselves.

The paper was white, and yellowed around the edges. In the middle, scrawled in black, was the message:

Please come find me
I am stranded
Small island, forty miles west of IDL
(The place where yesterday meets Tomorrow)
32 degrees latitude
David Millstone

"My goodness. We have to help this man," said Rayna.

"I don't think so," was Dad's reply.

"Why not?" I asked.

Dad pointed to something at the very bottom of the page that none of us had noticed yet.

It was dated October 8th, 1963.

It was way too late for us to help the poor man. We would never go to the island he described, and we would never meet anyone named David Millstone. But his note, written decades earlier, would finally give us the break we so desperately needed.

CHAPTER 3

Dinner and Riddles

That night we all met at our usual spot for dinner. The yacht came with a full crew, although they didn't mingle with us too much, and this included a chef. He was the best cook I'd ever come across, and I looked forward to every meal. So far, he'd only served peas once, and I made sure that he knew this was unacceptable. The entire staff, including the captain, was a mystery to me. Although they would end up seeing many strange things, they never really questioned why or how. And Joseph seemed to know more about them than he would let on.

The section of the ship where we ate was called the Mess Hall by the crew, and a massive wooden table and chairs filled the room and made it feel cramped. After the food was served (steak, shrimp, and potatoes) and we all dug in, Joseph kept talking about the note from the bottle, and how something from it was tugging at his memory, driving him crazy. We were no help, and soon Joseph drifted off into silent contemplation.

For the umpteenth time since our ocean quest had begun,

I looked around the huge round table at all of my companions. Mom sat next to me, a look of worry an absolute constant on her face. Rusty was next, devouring his third helping of steak and shrimp, oblivious to the line of sauce dripping off his chin. Then sat Dad, wondering aloud at the fate of poor Mr. Millstone, stuck on that island so many years ago.

Miyoko ate with quiet reserve next to my dad while her eyes remained fixed on an indeterminate point across the room. Her father, Tanaka, sat next to her, his lack of table manners matched only by his bad jokes. They, along with Rayna, were also members of The Alliance. I wondered again if either of them had special powers like some of the other members of that group.

Then there was The Hooded One. Hood. The man who couldn't speak, but painted with his finger. The man who could travel in an instant by way of a red hula hoop. The man who had been through so much, and who had become such a close friend. As had Rayna, sitting next to Hood. She had the ability to manipulate photographs to show the future. It could be a downright spooky gift.

Then there was Joseph. Twice we had lost him, and both times he had come back. We hoped that this was one thing that didn't end up coming in threes, like plane crashes. I still felt that Joseph knew a lot that he wasn't telling us about, but I tried not to push him too hard for information. Sometimes there was such a thing as too much knowledge, and it was enough burden just thinking about the next task in our mission: finding the Third Gift.

Captain Drake, or Tinkles, and the rest of his crew ate with us sometimes, but usually kept pretty much to themselves. I was glad for that, because it was very uncomfortable talking about things in front of them. Tanaka spoke, jostling me from my train of thought.

"Hey Jimmy-san, you seem very quiet tonight. Make it much harder for me to make funny jokes about stupid things you say. What's wrong?"

"Nothing." I took a sip of my drink. "I'm just thinking about all of us, and wondering if we're going to float in the ocean for the rest of our lives."

Tanaka was just about to spew forth an interminable comment when Joseph slammed his fist on the table and stood up, revelation spread all over his face. Everyone's dishes jumped and clattered at the sudden thump, and Mom yelped in surprise.

"Joseph," she said, "what's wrong?"

Without saying a word, he ran out of the room.

❧

"Ah!" Tanaka shouted, after Joseph left the Mess Hall. He pointed his finger up into the air. "Joseph no wait when he gotta go, neh?"

Not even sure we knew what Tanaka was talking about, a couple of us gave a slight courtesy laugh, but we were mostly enthralled by Joseph's strange behavior. Dad was just scooting his chair from the table to follow when Joseph sprang back into the room. The yellowed and dated note was in his hand, his face lit with excitement. He must have finally realized what had been nagging at his mind.

Joseph grabbed his chair, dragged it around the table, and placed it next to my dad. Then he went back to the door and yelled for Captain Tinkles to come down. Joseph came and sat next to Dad, and soon the captain joined us, wondering what in the heck all the fuss was about.

"Okay, okay." Joseph paused, and put his hands together and brought them to his lips, as if gathering his wits to explain something of great importance to all of us.

"All right, J.M., read this note again."

Joseph handed the note to my dad, and with a questioning look, Dad did as he was told.

"Uh, *please come find me . . . I am stranded . . . small island, blah, blah, blah, David Millstone.*"

Dad handed the note back to Joseph, who looked like Dad had just called him a big dumpy dopey head.

"Excuse me, Mr. J.M. Fincher, you just blah, blah, blahed over the one part that I intended to point out. Now come on, humor me for a second, and read it again. Geez, you're getting as bad as Tanaka the puke magnet over there." He jerked a thumb at Tanaka, who was trying his darnedest to retaliate with a comeback but, for once, came up empty.

Dad took the note back. "All right, sorry, it's just that we've all read this note a million times." He cleared his throat, and read the note word for word.

"*Please come find me . . . I am stranded . . . small island, 40 miles west of IDL . . . the place where yesterday meets tomorrow . . . 32 degrees latitude . . . David Millstone.*"

Joseph took the note back. "We have all been feeling sorry for this guy, knowing that we could do nothing for him. This is true—hopefully someone else saved him after he threw this bottle into the ocean. But we completely ignored his directions to the island on which he was stranded."

He sat back, and crinkled his brow, which set off an assortment of strange wrinkles on his hairless head.

"Okay," Dad said, "what are you saying? We should go to this island?"

"No, no, no, not at all." Joseph turned and looked at the captain. "Captain, uh, Tinkles," (Joseph was as uncomfortable with the silly name as I was), "we have all ignored the term 'IDL' that was in the note. Can you tell us what that means?"

"Well, that's easy, my friend." His voice was the sound of gravel being poured into a foundation. "It stands for International Date Line—some have given it the nickname that the note referred to. *The place where yesterday meets tomorrow.* His directions would make it very easy to spot the island he was stranded on."

Joseph stood up and began to pace around the table.

"International Date Line. Captain, explain to us what that means, what it is."

Tinkles acted happy to show off his wisdom on such things. "The IDL is the place in the world where the day officially changes from one to the next. In other words, it's where Sunday becomes Monday."

Rusty was confused, and asked the captain what he meant. Okay, I was confused, too, and was glad that Rusty spoke up.

"All right, lad, think about time changes and time zones. As you move west to east, it gets later and later, hour by hour, as you enter the next time zone, one by one, correct?"

Rusty nodded.

"Well, the world has twenty-four time zones. If you didn't have the International Date Line, you would just keep getting later and later as you continued to travel around the world, eh, for infinity? The IDL is the place in the world, a theoretically drawn line, defined and agreed upon by the countries of the world, where you actually switch days." The captain drew an invisible line in the air, and then pointed to one side of it. "On the east side of the Line, say it was noon on Monday." He pointed to the opposite side of his invisible line. "On the west side of the line, it would be noon on Tuesday. Oh . . . dolphin-burgers, I never realized how difficult it can be to explain."

Joseph slapped the captain on the back. "Nah, that was pretty darn good, actually. That's why some people call it 'the place where yesterday meets tomorrow.' Do you get it, Rusty? Jimmy? Tanaka?" Tanaka grumbled at being included with the kids in the question.

Rusty and I looked at each other, and then nodded. It seemed to make sense, although it was a bit confusing.

"Now for the kicker," Joseph said, a proud look on his face. It was the look of someone who had finally won Monopoly after a ten-hour marathon game. "What if you could literally stand on this theoretical line, straddle it, with one foot on one side, and the other foot on the other side?"

He was met with a mixture of looks, most of them confused.

"The Tower of Three Days, my friends. The tower where it can be three days at the same time."

I felt like things were almost making sense, but it still eluded me, like trying to see out of a frosted window in the car.

Dad interjected, also on the cusp of understanding.

"I can see where it could be two days at the same time, if

you straddled the line, I guess. But where are you getting the third day?"

"Well," Joseph replied, "it sounds crazy, but I'm confident that I'm right. Look." He sprung up onto the table, his head brushing the ceiling. There was a crack down the middle of the table, a place to separate if you wanted to move it. Joseph put his feet on opposite sides of the crack. He then gestured to each side.

"Okay, this side of me is Monday, where my right foot is, and this side of me is Tuesday, where my left foot is."

"Right, two days," said Dad.

"No, don't think of it that way!" Joseph replied, with a hint of frustration at not being able to explain himself as well as he would like. "To my left foot, the right foot is in 'yesterday.' To my right foot, the left foot is in 'tomorrow.' To both feet, they think they are in 'today.' Yesterday, today, and tomorrow. My body would be in all three days at the same time. If this 'Tower' straddles the International Date Line, it would be as well. We know the Tower is in the ocean, where most of the IDL is located."

We stared, letting it sink in. It seemed to click for all of us at the same time. Joseph was right. How could yesterday meet tomorrow without a today squeezed in the middle? He jumped down off the table.

"I say we head for the Line and travel along its path. Hopefully we'll meet the Tower of Three Days more sooner than later. Sound feasible, Captain?"

"Aye. It would be easy to maintain a path traveling along the Line. I'll alter our course right away."

The words were barely out of the captain's mouth before everything changed in a chilling instant.

A frightful scream came from above, on the decks. It was the terrified yell of one of the crew. Without hesitation, we all headed for the door and climbed the short staircase out into the open air.

The night was dark, more so than usual because of a storm that had begun to creep into the area. The air was wet with mist. The man screamed again, and we saw him standing near the railing on the far side of the boat, pointing to the sky.

We could not see the object of his frightened attention.

But a sudden and dreadful sound filled the air. I felt my heart pause before it set to racing.

It was the clanking sound of metallic teeth.

CHAPTER 4

The Chain Gang

Captain Tinkles sprinted to the main cabin, and seconds after he entered, the place blazed to life with lights. Like dawn on a battlefield, the light brought forth the horrors of the day. In staggered silence, we stared at the skies above us.

From the cloudy north, a writhing entity was approaching, a rolling black cloud of shifting shapes. At first it looked like a disorganized mass of limbs and shadow and wings and eyes. Long, rope-like things were waving back and forth, hanging from the bottom of the cloud.

Then, the cloud separated, and took on definition.

Gray and black creatures with wings. Bodies that were trapped somewhere between human and beast, wings outstretched behind them, black as onyx, flapping with determination and purpose. Eddies of mist were spreading behind each creature as they approached. Black eyes stared out of gray faces.

The Shadow Ka.

There was no longer any doubt concerning the words of Raspy, spoken in the Pointing Finger, that the Ka were *evolving.* In the weeks since our last confrontation, that evolution had seemed to quicken. It wouldn't be long before these hybrids of human and Ka were the full-fledged beasts of shadow I had encountered in the Blackness. Squeezing fists of hopeless fear made my stomach twist, and I wanted to sink to my knees.

Their skin was gray, with thick, black veins stretching and branching throughout, as if the shadow substance was taking over bit by bit. Their eyes were an empty black, and parts of their body seemed to shimmer now and then, looking empty for an instant before coming back again. My eyes were having a difficult time convincing my brain that they weren't fibbing, that these things were really there, coming at us with an inexplicable hate.

As they approached, the source of the rattling, metallic clatter became clear. Each Ka had a long chain wrapped around its neck, the two ends swaying back and forth, banging into each other, making an eerie clanking sound.

The first Ka landed on the ship, its feet coming down with a soft thump, the ends of its chain banging loudly then rattling as it slid to a stop. The Ka folded its wings back until they almost disappeared and then looked around with vengeance in its eyes. Others soon followed, the thumping sounds of their grotesque feet and the disturbing rattle of the chains accompanying them. The folding of their wings made a soft airy sound, like a paper fan being folded and put away.

I didn't notice the lack of their trademark scream until a Ka finally let one out with a piercing screech, which reminded me all too well. The other Ka seemed to answer as one, and soon the thunderous noise of their cries blistered the air.

Twenty or so had landed, with many more staying in

the air, circling the yacht like vultures awaiting their prey to finally die before coming in for the feast. The thought made me quiver as I realized that just might be the case.

The spectacle before us must have been as hypnotic as it was terrifying, because not one of us had moved a muscle since coming out into the open, except for the captain, who had never returned from the main cabin. I looked around me. My heart leapt into my throat.

Every one of my companions, everyone, had their eyes closed, swaying back and forth like pine trees in the wind. Rayna and my dad collapsed to the deck, falling limp and rolling over like dropped rag dolls. Then my mom fell. Then Rusty. The terror and confusion of seeing them drop made a bile soup in my gut. Tanaka fell. Miyoko fell. They all lay there like it was afternoon nap time, although their positions didn't look very comfortable.

Finally, Joseph fell.

I looked back at the Shadow Ka, one of whom was walking toward me, a wicked grin splitting his gray, vein-filled face. Then the strangest thing happened.

I felt an overwhelming urge to go to sleep.

❦

A black haze appeared before my eyes, spots of all colors dancing in the shadows. Every part of me wanted nothing but the quiet escape of slumber, to lie down right then and there and fall fast asleep. My knees became weak, and I felt the fear drain out of me.

The Shadow Ka stopped three feet in front of me. I could barely make him out, my vision giving in to the desire to rest.

The Ka screamed. It had a strange pitch—different from any other time I'd heard it.

I don't recall if I had ever been quite so close to one when it screamed. The violent sound exploded through my head, ripping the sleepy feeling out of me in an instant, like being doused with ice water to keep you awake. I was left with no trace of the strange sensation—it was completely gone. I was wide awake, back in the clutches of fear.

I looked down. Everyone was awake, pushing themselves up into a standing position, their faces creased with confusion.

The Shadow Ka spoke. Its voice was harsh and low, with a slight sneer to it.

"Not yet. No, not yet. The time for that will come soon enough."

His words made no sense, but the evil in them was palpable.

"You are Jimmy Fincher?" he asked me, his tone revealing that it was a rhetorical question. "I have a proposal. We are here to take you and your comrades back with us. Will you come, or will you make this difficult?"

So much for introductions.

Instead of answering, I blew him off the ship with a swift burst of Ice, the second Gift I had received from the Givers. It no longer took effort, only thought. Exploding from my hand with a swoosh of frosty air, the solid block of ice formed and crashed into him, hurtling him hundreds of feet out into the ocean. We heard no splash.

An instant later, the remaining Ka took off into the air, their great wings creating a miniature hurricane as they all beat in urgent unison. In seconds, they were gone into the mist, their screams dulled by the wet air.

As they left, I thought about what the leader had said. They had come to negotiate? It made no sense, but my use of the Ice had been the definitive answer they'd not wanted. So they left in a rush of dark wind.

But we knew they would be back.

CHAPTER 5

Sleeping Disorders

A few minutes later, we were gathered in the Mess Hall again, with two main topics to discuss. One, the surprise visit from our archenemy. Two, what on earth happened out there with the sleepy thing? Its oddness was only matched by how unsettling it was. What if the Ka had developed some strange method of hypnosis?

"Let's talk about what we all felt right before we collapsed to the ground," Dad said. "I know for me, it all happened very fast. A sudden surge of fear ripped through my body when I saw that first half-man, half-Ka thing land on our ship, and the next thing I knew, blackness filled my vision and I was falling. It was like my whole system just shut down—like someone flipped off my power switch."

"Same for me," said Miyoko. Her voice revealed a slight twinge of doom, like she could not make herself recover from the ordeal. As it was, she had been so quiet all night that I couldn't help but wonder if something was troubling her, something besides what had just happened outside.

Joseph spoke next. "For me it was when I heard the first

26

scream. It brought back the memory of the Blackness, when I was taken by that hoard of Ka when you blocked the Black Curtain, Jimmy." He looked at me, his face pale from the memory. "It reminded me of that horrible place—the black, gooey face. My heart almost stopped from fear, and then everything faded into darkness. I don't remember falling."

Tanaka coughed, and made a gesture to let us know he was speaking next. Despite the circumstances, or, knowing Tanaka, perhaps because of them, he made his best attempt at a joke.

"I thought I know meaning of ugly when I met Jimmy for first time." He grinned in my direction. "But those . . . things got him beat, I'm sorry to say. It was the sight of their gray skin, and those black lines all over—that's what scared me so badly. And then the dark came over me, like the world had been sucked away with a snap of the fingers. It was . . . so strange."

A dark pall washed over Tanaka's face, something I never thought I would see. It made me want to cry and give up to see someone with such a cheerful demeanor suddenly look so dejected.

"I don't remember much," said Rayna. "The last thing I remember is hearing that terrible cry of the Ka again. I don't remember falling. Hooded One, what was it like for you?"

Hood had been very quiet as well, which was saying a lot, considering he doesn't talk. His frayed robe hung from his body, looking sadder than usual. His faceless head jerked up at the mention of his name, and he stood and held up a wooden board he had taken to carrying around for messages. The paint from his finger washed clean from it pretty easily. Hood pointed his pinkie finger and placed it on the board, then revealed once again his otherworldly gift.

He began to paint words with nothing but his finger.

"IT WAS AS IF THE ONE CALLED RASPY HAD RETURNED." He turned the board over. "I, TOO, FELL INTO DARKNESS." He sat back down, and I realized he had his red ring, The Bender Ring, at his side for support. Hood and I had once traveled many miles, from a riverside mansion to a mountainside shack, in a matter of seconds by going through that ring. I would never forget the sensation of the rushing redness when we did it.

Mom was sitting next to me, and when she began to speak, I could see that she had been crying. "Every time I think the horror cannot get any worse, something new happens. Those things were something out of a child's nightmare. My stomach turned at the sight of that veined skin, and the black eyes, the wings . . ." She wiped her eyes with her sleeve. "I don't remember anything, really. Just fear and darkness coming over me."

"What about you, Rusty?" Dad asked.

"I don't know," he said. "For some reason I was worried about Jimmy. I knew he had his Gifts, but I just, I don't know, got really scared again that they were going to figure out a way past those Gifts and take him." He looked at me. "Let's face it, Jimmy is the only one they really want. I had this surge of something, I don't know, fear or whatever, that they were just gonna scoop up my *dweebish* little brother and take off. Then I felt really tired. Then I fell."

"Did you just call me *dweebish*?" I asked. "What exactly does that mean, anyway?"

"It means reeking little boys who run off and get special powers so their brothers can't beat the crud out of them anymore."

Everyone tried to laugh, but it was very weak. It was almost as lame as some of our courtesy laughs for Tanaka in the past.

"Anyway, monkey-boy," Rusty said, "what happened with you? Why didn't you pass out?"

"Well, I did get this weird feeling like I wanted to go to sleep. But it happened way after you guys—I saw all of you fall down."

"Were you very scared?" asked Rayna. "As scared as we were?"

I thought for a second. "No, not really. But remember, I have the Shield, and I've met up with these things over and over now. But I was scared a little, I guess, because the more people we gather, the more difficult it's going to be to do our little trick with hugging." The Shield was my first gift, the one that protects me from anything and everything. When others are in direct contact with me, the Shield expands and protects them as well. It had helped my family more than once, but there was just no way we could have everyone on the yacht touching me at the same time.

"I was more scared for you guys than for me," I continued. "Why do you ask?"

Rayna frowned. "I can't say for sure. I'm working on a theory somewhere in my head, but I don't want to talk about it until I have more time to think on it."

"Well," Dad said, "we better get some rest; it's pretty late."

He looked at his watch. "We've kind of slacked off in having consistent lookouts while we sleep. I think we'd all agree that we can no longer afford to be careless with that. Everyone get in bed, and I'll take first watch. Then Joseph can take a turn in a few hours."

"That's fine, J.M.," Joseph said, "but what are we going to do if they come again? Heck, *when* they come again."

Dad stood up. "Good point. Jimmy, I think I better turn this question over to you." Dad walked over and put his hands on my shoulders and squeezed—that universal sign from dads that they love you. "But, I doubt they'll come again tonight. Let's all get some rest, and we'll come up with a plan of action tomorrow."

"What if they do come tonight, Dad?" Rusty asked.

Dad smiled.

"Run to Jimmy."

"Glad to know it's all up to me," I said.

"Come on, we'll be all right. It's not like we're a bunch of wimps, right? Except for that old geezer Tanaka sitting over there."

Tanaka stood up and roared his displeasure. "Mister Fincher-san, you ask your boy about that, neh?" Once, Tanaka had lifted me above his head and spun me around with barely any effort at all.

"All right, all right, you win, Mr. Tanaka. Come on, let's go to bed. Those things aren't coming tonight, and if they do, Jimmy will get rid of them in a jiffy."

Dad would prove to be wrong on both counts.

CHAPTER 6

Veins and Chains

It was just past midnight, the soft drizzle of the unabated storm sending a quiet but constant echo of pitter-patter throughout the ship's quarters. Low clouds hung over the yacht like a dome of wet cotton, rebounding all sound, creating the strange sensation of being indoors. On the deck of the ship, the world was grim.

Dad had felt certain that the adrenaline rush of the evening would keep him awake for hours. He sat in a lawn chair on the topmost deck, peering into the night with a feeling like he was all alone in the world. Although he would not quite admit it to himself, he knew that somewhere inside of him he was terrified that the Shadow Ka would return before morning, before we had the time and energy to devise a plan of defense. There were just so many of them.

While we all slept below, Dad sat at his post, guardian of the fortress.

Twenty minutes later, defying his fear, he fell asleep.

Rusty and I shared a cabin, a simple room with a window, two small beds, a dresser and a closet. The gentle rocking of the boat had been pure misery for my stomach the first couple of weeks, but now it had become a soothing sensation, and mixed with the gentle rain, better than any sleeping pill.

I was in the depths of slumber, having some bizarre dream about Superman asking me to take over for him while he went to visit his in-laws in Africa, when something woke me up.

The sounds of the chains were descending upon us once again.

The clanging thud of them clattering along the outside of my cabin was like dragging a string of bones across glass. The Ka were back, and they were up to something with those chains. Fear washed the sleep away like a high-powered fire hose on a single mote of dust. Half a second after I heard the grating sound of the chains, I was standing at the small round window, wide-awake. Condensation made it impossible to see anything but liquid drops of crystal, and I turned to run out the door.

After a quick shove to wake Rusty up, I made for the hallway and the short stairs that led up to the main deck.

Up above, everything had gone bonkers.

The lights were out, so it was difficult to see anything but dark shapes and shifting shadows from the scant moonlight seeping through the overcast sky like an old werewolf movie. But the piercing sound of throaty roars and dragging chain links left no doubt that the Shadow Ka were back. And they were very busy.

It was impossible to tell what they were doing, but they had an obvious air of intent. The chains. What was the deal with the chains?

No one else was around, and I wondered who had been on watch. Dad should have awakened the next person by then, but I didn't see him or anyone else. I was torn. Should I begin defending us from the Ka, start shooting Ice at them like a crazed Jack Frost, or should I gather everyone and come up with a quick plan? Conflicting thoughts and confusion ran through my head, and I just sat there for several seconds.

A Ka screamed near my head. The sound of a chain whipping through the air, and a gust of wind brushed my hair as the Ka flew past me. It didn't bother messing with me, knowing about the Shield. It landed several feet from me, and I could just see the outline of the human shape with wings attached, a long chain hanging around its neck. It looked at me and screamed again.

Then it started wrapping the long chain around something, I couldn't tell what. At first I panicked, thinking it was my dad, but it wasn't a person. I looked around, straining my eyes. The Ka were everywhere, some flapping their wings, hovering to the sides of the ship, many more all over the ship itself. All of them were doing things with their chains, wrapping them, twisting them, tying them.

I yelled out, asking if anyone else was up there. No answer.

I ran back down the stairs. Rusty was standing at the doorway to our small cabin, looking terrified.

"Jimmy, what's happening? What are they doing out there?"

"I don't know. They're wrapping their chains around things, fastening and securing them. It doesn't make any sense."

"Is anyone else up there?" he asked.

"Not that I can tell. Stay here, I'll try to get everybody together."

Rusty went and sat down on his bed, his face full of worry.

I had just turned to run to the next door when Rusty yelped, a wail of surprise. I halted and popped my head back in our room.

"Look!" Rusty yelled. He pointed at our small window, the one that looked out on the ocean, with no railings or walkways below it.

Dad was out there, staring at us.

Then he was gone.

CHAPTER 7

Dad in a Pickle

I ran to the window and looked out, but the glass was too thick, making peripheral views impossible. Dad was nowhere in sight. Then a dark shadow flashed past, then flew by again. Something sparkled as it went by the second time, and I was almost positive it was my dad's wedding ring. One of the Ka had my dad in its clutches.

My stomach now turning with a sick sense of dread, I ran out of the room and started shouting. Behind me, Rusty was yelling, "They've got Dad! They've got Dad!"

My family loved to accentuate the obvious.

By now, others had appeared, and after a few moments of confusion, we were all gathered inside the Mess Hall. Dad was the only one missing, and Mom was a wreck. Captain Tinkles told us that he had tried to turn the lights on but nothing happened. They must have busted them while going about their strange task out there so everything would remain dark.

Rayna took charge.

"Jimmy, you go out there right now and get your dad. Don't worry about us; we'll figure things out. Go, go!"

Wondering where my newfound courage of recent weeks had gone, I nodded and made for the door. Miyoko ran up to me.

"Jimmy, I'll go with you."

"What?"

"Come on!" She grabbed my elbow.

I pulled it out of her grip. "Miyoko, are you crazy? Just stay here."

"Child of the Gifts, take her with you," Tanaka said.

I looked at him, waiting for his punch line, but none came. His face was set in stone. I turned back to Miyoko. She grabbed my hand this time.

"I have yet to reveal something to you. Let's go."

She pulled me after her. As we went though the door, I asked her what she meant.

"I am a member of the Alliance, Jimmy." She stopped long enough to look at me. "We all have our own . . . talents."

She turned and ran, pulling me along once again. As we burst out into the open air, she yelled one more thing before the chaos began.

"Just don't you dare let go of me!"

⟨❦⟩

It was still very dark, and the captain had been right. Not a light to be seen. We could see nothing but mist and shadow. But they were out there. We could hear them moving, and hear the echoing rattle of the chains.

"What are we supposed to do? I can't see anything!"

Miyoko did not reply, and I looked down at her face. I could barely make out her features, enough to see that her eyes were closed. She was mumbling something, and panic tickled my innards, remembering how everyone had fainted the last time we were in this situation.

"Miyoko! Wake up!" I squeezed her hand.

"Huh?" She squeezed back, but did not open her eyes. "Oh. No, no. It's not that. Just hold on for a minute."

The mumbling began again as I wondered what on the planet she was doing.

"Okay," she said after another few seconds. "Turn your head and close your eyes."

"Turn my—"

"Just do it!"

I looked the other way, into the darkness, and closed my eyes.

When I was a kid (okay, when I was a *little* kid), my mom would always wake me up for school in stages. First, she would just open the door and call my name out. She knew that this would never work, but it started the process. Then, after about ten minutes, she would come in and shake me and tell me it was time to get up. Then, after another few minutes, she would turn on the lights. The blast of the lights through my eyelids always did the trick in jerking the sleep out of my brain.

What happened right then was just like that.

Only it was a hundred times worse.

A piercing arrow of light shattered the darkness completely, and despite having my eyes closed, I felt sure that I was blinded forever.

Miyoko was yelling.

"Don't look at me! The light from my eyes will blind you! But now . . . but now you can see. Let's find your dad. Just DO NOT look into my eyes!"

I opened mine, and for a few seconds, the world seemed to be a winter wonderland, white spots everywhere. Every sense in my body urged me to look at Miyoko, to see what this power of hers could be that lights up the universe, but I resisted. It reminded me of that place under the Pointing Finger, when I had to avoid looking at the rift behind me in order to obtain the Second Gift.

My eyes adjusted, and I took it all in. Brilliant light permeated our surroundings, seeming to drive the mist and darkness away. The ship was loaded with Shadow Ka, their moist, gray, veined skin reflecting the light in distorted insanity. Most had their wings folded, and they waited, and watched. Many shielded their eyes, and some looked afraid, an emotion I had never seen on them before.

I sprang into action, and looked for whichever beast held my dad in its gray clutches. Still holding Miyoko's hand, this time it was me who dragged her along. I could not let go of her, or else she'd lose the protection of the Shield, but I also wanted her behind me so that I would not look into the source of the blinding light. In my head, I imagined oval orbs of light where her eyes should be, blasting forth their luminescence like the spotlights so common at grand openings and car shows.

The Ka did nothing as I ran around, completely indifferent to my search. It was unnerving to see them this way. I wondered what it was they awaited. Each one had a chain still around its neck, the ends dropping down tightly and wrapped around various parts of the ship-railings, beams, and parts of the actual structure.

A thought began to form in my mind. *Were they actually intending to . . . ?*

My dad's voice broke my line of concentration.

He was screaming my name, the volume increasing steadily, like he was falling from the sky . . . I looked up. A Shadow Ka was swooping down from above, my dad in its grip, its gray arms and legs holding him firmly. It swooped to within a few feet of me, then headed out to sea. A gale of wind from its passing blew in my face, carrying the reek of body odor and sewage filth. Forty or fifty feet from the yacht, with all the care of a man taking out his garbage, the Ka dumped my dad into the dark waters. The light from Miyoko's eyes revealed the ocean swallowing him whole.

He did not come back up.

CHAPTER 8

Bath in Dirty Water

I knew this was another trap, but I had no choice, absolutely no choice. Not knowing what else to do with Miyoko but take her along for her protection, I squeezed her hand, closed my eyes to avoid being blinded, leaned over toward her ear, and told her what we had to do. To my surprise, she didn't complain.

We ran to the railing on that side of the boat, and we both climbed onto it, swinging our feet up and over until we were sitting on the topmost part, our feet dangling on the side toward the ocean. I told Miyoko to grab onto my neck.

Then I called upon the Ice.

With a thought, I pushed a stream of ice into the waters below me and then *willed* it to expand and continue outward in a wide path toward the place where my dad had fallen. The waters of the ocean intermingled with the misty air swirling into Ice, and in seconds the frozen walkway I'd envisioned had formed. Before the ship could drift away from the flat iceberg I'd created, Miyoko and I jumped onto the hard, frosty trail. It was a decent fall, but the Shield protected us, and a bounce or two later we were running down the icy trail, slipping and sliding the whole way. It took all my effort to not look into her eyes.

We skidded to a stop at the end, and looked down, the worry for my dad increasing with every passing second. I imagined him encased in water, not breathing. Before I could blink an eye, Miyoko let go of my hand, and dove into the ocean, headfirst.

I tried to stop her, but she was gone. For a frantic second, I hesitated, some fear of sharks and sea monsters bubbling up from nightmares past. Then, I followed her.

But I went feet first like a scaredy-cat.

❧❧

The waters enveloped me like a blanket of slushy ice. It was freezing, and ripped the breath from my lungs. It didn't feel wet so much as it felt like cold, biting pinpricks of steel. Every control function in my body went into panic mode, and seemed to shut down. I felt a rising terror that I would never breathe again.

When my eyes instinctively opened, seconds after the plunge, stinging pain shut them right up. I opened them again, just barely, squinting in an attempt to shield them from the salt and minerals in the water. It still hurt, but there was no choice but to endure it.

A great light was scanning the ocean around us, penetrating the dark and murky waters like a flashlight through smoky air. I turned to the source but stopped just in time, natural warning beacons going off in my head, just as if you accidentally looked at the sun. It was Miyoko, looking for my dad.

My brain was growing tired as I thrashed at the waters, trying to look where the light went. I needed air. With no power to fight that urge, I broke the surface and gasped, sucking in as much water as oxygen. The taste of it, the volume of it, gagged me like someone had shoved a thick towel down my throat. Wracking coughs exploded from me, and it took every ounce of effort to tread the water.

Then, the Shield kicked in.

CHAPTER 9

Bubble Submarine

Weeks ago, when we had entered the frozen world through an iron gate in the Blackness, we had been buffeted by snow and wind. The Shield had done nothing until the cold had started to hurt me, and then it sprung into action and repelled everything, like an invisible bubble. That same sort of thing happened again. Not all things that are harmful to a person are cut and dry, immediately discernible. The Shield seemed to have its own brain. In fact, according to Farmer, the Giver who had helped me so much in this ordeal, the Shield's brain was *my* brain.

Just as despair filled my heart, as I choked and sputtered and slapped at the water, a sudden and silent explosion of air shot from me in all directions, pushing the water away until a pocket of emptiness completely surrounded me. I fell a few feet and bounced on the inside bottom of the bubble until I came to a tenuous stop, still wobbling slightly. I looked up, and realized it wasn't a bubble at all. The pocket of air separated the waters at the surface in a perfect circle, so that I looked like I was standing in a glass cup, ten feet tall, floating in the ocean.

The sensation of being surrounded by water, held back by some invisible force, as I bobbed up and down, was nauseating. But it beat choking on salty seawater and dying.

I got down on my knees, floating and bobbing on what looked like a super-strong film of plastic wrap, or some invisible skin of ocean pudding. I crawled along, and the Shield went with me, the pocket of air going wherever I went, the invisible barrier wet but impenetrable.

The light from Miyoko's eyes was just a few feet below me, still moving, or I would've thought her dead for sure. It had to have been a couple of minutes by then. She seemed to be struggling with something. Her head was jerking left and right, not like she was looking for something but instead trying to swim to the surface with a heavy burden. Dad. She had my dad.

I dove for them.

The Shield acted strangely as I descended, kind of alternating between repelling the water and letting me dive into it. Waves of water hit me then were pushed away, almost like I was swimming through soft, wet clay. It was exhausting, pushing and pulling, pushing and pulling myself toward them.

Miyoko seemed to slow, then her movements ceased completely. She was giving up, refusing to leave Dad behind, but also refusing to save herself. Her light grew dim, then winked out.

I screamed, and dove with a burst of effort summoned from the deepest part of my heart. I tore through the remaining distance and grabbed her. Dad was held in her weakening grip. With both arms, I hugged them to me. The Shield expanded to protect all of us, forming what was now a complete bubble, fully encased in the black waters.

Miyoko coughed and spat, gasping for life.

Dad did not move or make a sound.

There wasn't enough water in the ocean to match the heaviness that gripped my heart when I saw him.

He looked for all the world like a dead man.

CHAPTER 10

Unexpected Departure

With some bizarre mixture of crying and yelling, I held on to them and kicked toward the surface. Going up was much easier than going down, the Shield almost pushing me up. We surfaced just a few feet away from the long icy landing that led back to the ship. The invisible cup of my protection kind of rolled along under my feet as I half carried, half drug Miyoko and Dad to the ice platform I had created earlier. Miyoko regained enough of her strength to help, or it would have been impossible.

Dad wasn't showing any signs of life. We lifted him up and onto the ice, then climbed onto it ourselves. The ocean water held back by my Shield sloshed against the ice as the force of my Gift left it. The most amazing thing about the whole ordeal was that it was *no longer* amazing. The Shield had truly become a part of me.

"Here, help me roll him over," Miyoko said.

We did so with a grunt, and his arm flopped over and slapped the ice as he settled onto his back. His skin was pale and wet, his hair matted to his head like seaweed. I realized

46

I was sobbing, trying to tell myself that he couldn't be dead. Miyoko looked at me, her eyes back to normal again.

"Jimmy," she said, putting her hand on my arm. "He is not dead." She pointed at his chest. "Look."

I blinked the tears away and followed her gaze.

Dad was breathing.

I could never explain the feeling that came over me at that moment. Dad meant more to me than any words in any language could ever begin to describe. He was my father, my hero, my friend, my everything. For a full minute, as we had struggled to get out of the ocean and onto the ice, my brain told me that he was dead. To see that proven false, to see his chest rising and falling in a regular pattern, was like the universe itself exploding within me, life and love and happiness washing over me like dawn finally breaking on a thousand years of darkness.

The strength of angels and soldiers filled me, and I stood up.

"Come on," I said, bending over and reaching out my hand. "Let's get rid of those dang Shadow Ka."

We grabbed my dad and lifted, each putting a shoulder under one of his arms, and headed down the ice, back to our ship. Dad's dragging feet left shallow trenches in the frosty path.

The flat iceberg was a lot longer than I remembered. My family could've filled a book with all the jokes we'd come up with over the years about my dad's ever increasing pant size, but right then it didn't seem so funny. It felt like he weighed a ton, and the occasional grunt that escaped his lips now and then only made it worse, like he was having a hoot seeing us struggle to carry and drag him. I promised myself to buy him a treadmill with Joseph's new money when all this was over.

Halfway there, we took a small break, dropping Dad like a sack of potatoes.

It was then that I realized the sky had grown considerably lighter. Miyoko's eye-lights had long been extinguished, yet we could see pretty well. I looked up and saw that the clouds were dissipating a bit, and the full moon shone through a break in the sky, although a strange haze seemed to filter it, like a thick screen on a window. There was something odd about it, but I was too tired to sort it out. I pushed the thought aside, and looked toward our destination.

The yacht waited for us, the dark shapes of the Shadow Ka still scattered all over it, still standing at their posts, wings folded. A few still flew around the ship, but most were on the boat itself, chains tied to something, waiting. There had to be at least fifty of them. I saw no sign of my family, the Alliance, or the crew, and hoped against hope that they were safe, locked inside.

I motioned to Miyoko and we picked Dad up and headed once again down the iceberg.

"What exactly are we going to do when we get back up there?" she asked. "We're heavily outnumbered, and all I can do is blind a few of them."

Panting from the effort of dragging my dad's gargantuan body, I looked over at her and tried to smile.

"I fully intend on ice-blasting me some Shadow Ka tonight."

Her half-hearted laugh cut short when her gaze shifted back to the waiting ship. The look on her face stopped my heart, and I turned to look as well. We stood and watched as a sound filled the air like a thousand bed sheets, hung to dry on a clothesline, flapping in the wind.

The yacht was lifting out of the water. Our ship, our boat, was taking flight.

The Shadow Ka were flying away, taking the yacht, and everyone on board, with them.

CHAPTER 11

Flying Dutchman

At first, what we were seeing did not register properly, the impossibility of it overwhelming our own sense of sight. Large ocean-going sea vessels do not fly. They float. Yet the yacht we had called home for over a month was rising, already five or six feet, the dark waters of the ocean streaming down its sides in sheets and rivulets. A hundred black wings beat against the night air.

Miyoko and I could not speak. Stunned, we quickened our pace, our adrenaline seeming to shed pounds from my dad's weight. I scanned the length of the ship, once more taking in the surreal sight of winged beasts carrying a huge boat. The purpose of the chains was no longer in doubt, nor was the strength of the Ka.

We were only feet away, the beginnings of the inward curving slope from the side of the ship, indicating the bottom, breaking the surface behind a curtain of cascading water. The weight of such a ship must be staggering, and I could not believe these things could just tie up some chains and fly off with it. But it appeared to be working just fine.

Without a word, Miyoko and I knew that we had to get on that ship or risk never seeing it again.

"Here," I yelled, "Help me get Dad in an upright position!"

We pushed under his armpits until he was almost standing, and then I put one hand under each of his arms while Miyoko strained with all her effort to keep him from falling down. Then I called upon the Ice.

Beams of it shot from my hands into his armpits, lifting him up toward the boat. The railing was a good twenty or thirty feet above us now, but I just didn't know what else to do. Every part of my brain riveted on the Gift, concentrating on the Ice gripping Dad and carrying him upward, shooting him toward the decks of the boat. The two beams expanded as he rose, defying gravity, pushing him, catapulting him.

When he rose above the railings, I twisted my thoughts and the Ice bent and careened forward, throwing my dad onto the ship. A sick thud sounded from above. He'd landed somewhere, hopefully not too hard.

Clear of the sucking waters of the ocean, the boat seemed to take off just after Dad landed, drastically increasing the speed of its ascent. In seconds the bottom of the yacht was above our heads and soaring upward.

"Miyoko," I yelled again, "grab onto me and hang on!"

She put her arms around my neck, and I motioned for her to swing around to my back, as if I were giving her a piggyback ride. She squeezed her arms and jumped onto me, placing her legs over my hips. Or, where a person should have hips. My skin and bones body had about as much hips as it did muscle, which ain't much. Her legs slipped to the ground.

"Try again," I said, frantic as I saw the ship getting higher and higher. It was now forty feet above us, twisting to take off in another direction. The few Shadow Ka not chained to the boat were barking their strange commands, guiding the others where to go.

Miyoko jumped up again, and this time I froze her legs to my hips with Ice, then froze her hands together so they could not slip from her grip around my neck.

I looked up, then closed my eyes for the briefest of moments while I imagined what I wanted the Ice to do. I looked up again, and concentrated my vision on the ladder that was attached to the very back of the yacht, put there for people to climb down in case something went wrong with the rudders or engines.

It was fifty feet above us.

A blasting stream of Ice shot from both my hands, clasped tightly together, wispy frost and mist swirling in a great tornado, barreling forward until its end reached the ladder. It expanded and covered several rungs of the ladder in a swath of solid Ice, keeping its hold on me at the other end of the cold rope, down below, fraught with anxiety, hoping it worked.

It ripped us into the air with a jerk, taking my breath away, the force of it making Miyoko's ice-bound hands slam against my throat. The Shield kicked in just enough to stop it from hurting.

The ship headed for the clouds, a long pillar of Ice hanging from its rear, a cold string of hope to the two people dangling from its end.

❦

The Shadow Ka flapped their wings with a strained urgency, appearing to bear a burden like never before in their evil lives. I thought it interesting that they flew the boat front-first, like it actually mattered once it was in the air. Once out of the water, they could have flown sideways or backward just as easily. But the ship tore through the wet air with purpose and direction, like the waters of the sea had merely risen in a great wave, carrying the yacht forward on a final and great voyage. We looked like the trailing anchor, no use at all, dragging against nothing but clouds.

I got my senses in order and started the shrinking process.

The fifty-foot-long rope of Ice shortened, slowly at first, then quickening its pace. White, swirling air cycloned off the beam as it shrank, its moisture disappearing back into the atmosphere. The rush from the shrinking frozen water combined with the ascending ship itself to make it seem as if we were a fighter jet, rocketing toward the edges of space and sound.

Forty feet, thirty, twenty, the backside of the ship suddenly loomed before us. I slowed the pace of shrinking, worried that if we hit it too hard, the Shield would tilt the ship as it rebounded to protect me.

The beam of Ice had shortened to about ten feet. The rungs of the ladder were right there, so close, the distance now less than the height of a basketball hoop.

Then the Shadow Ka attacked us in a rage of furious hate.

CHAPTER 12

The Shadow Storm

It appeared that most of the Ka were occupied with the task of hauling the boat, hoisting their share of the burden with their individual chains. But the horde that attacked us at that moment was like a storm of shadows, more than we could count. The ship tilted slightly, as if some of the Ka had indeed let go to help in the fight.

They came from all directions, and soon our vision was filled with flashing images of black and gray. The beating of their wings and the sound of their screeching howls contended with each other to dominate the air. The thin membrane of their wings flexed and pulled, glistening with moisture. My stomach turned. The dark chasms that were their eyes stared at us with a ferocious loathing.

Yet they did nothing to us.

They couldn't. The power of the Shield was no longer a secret to them, and they didn't even try, didn't even approach our immediate vicinity. But they swarmed around us, creating a swirling cloud of darkness, like a tornado of maddened black butterflies.

Miyoko held on, her hands bound in Ice, legs frozen to my sides. There was nothing she could do but watch. There was nothing I could do but watch. There were so many of them that I just felt overwhelmed, not knowing what good it would do to start shooting beams of Ice.

Distracted by their vicious appearance, I had stopped shrinking our rope, fooled once again by illusion, thinking that I could not get past them to the boat. I had to remind myself for the millionth time that the Shield pretty much allowed me to do whatever I wanted.

With a deep effort of thought, I willed the Ice to shrink the remaining ten feet, to take us straight through the writhing crowd of Ka.

We had gone about two feet when I fell asleep.

CHAPTER 13

Superman in Reverse

We've all had that feeling before. So many times I can remember being in school the day after staying up late to watch a football game or a movie, and just being exhausted. Class would be miserable, no matter the topic, and beckoning strings of sleep would pull at your eyelids all day. Every second you imagine how nice it would be just to curl up on the ground and take a power nap. Then it hits you.

Your head jerks, the world seems to bend in on itself for a split second, and you realize that you just fell asleep for an instant. It's a peculiar feeling, almost like you'd just served a secret mission for the government and had your memory erased.

Except for the slow building up of exhaustion, that moment of instantaneous falling asleep and jerking awake again is exactly what it felt like as we closed the final gap between the boat and us. Something inexplicable, in the middle of all that insanity, made me fall asleep. It could not have been more than a second before my head snapped up from its descent to my chest in its quest for peaceful slumber.

But we were already falling—small, sparkling jewels of shattered Ice our only company. The Ka had shattered the rope during my very brief and very unexplainable nap.

Falling was no new thing for me. The absence of fear was like a vacuum—I knew that I should be scared, and yet that feeling didn't even register in my mind. The only thing that kicked in was an immediate sense of calculation. The methods, the inner workings of my mind had changed so much since that fateful day in the woods. It didn't seem possible that it had only been a matter of months since it all began. It felt like years.

The oddest thing was that I was having these thoughts while plummeting toward the ocean with a girl frozen to my back, my friends and family growing smaller and smaller in the distance.

I shook myself mentally.

The chance of shooting Ice at the ship to reestablish a connection had come and gone before I could react. Gravity is a powerful thing. The distance between the ship and us had increased at a mind-numbing pace, and the boat already had grown small and insubstantial in the clouds.

Wind and rain whipped at us as we fell, our backs pointing down, our eyes facing the departing ship. I didn't know how high up we had gone, but I could feel the ocean below, coming to meet us at a blistering speed. There was not much time before we would burst into the waters like a stone bubble, protected but lost to the sea forever. I had two wonderful Gifts, but flying or radio communication was not one of them. I had two . . .

Then it came to me as an image, a vision in my mind. A plan.

It just might work . . .

CHAPTER 14

Every Child's Fantasy

The Shield deflected harmful things, be it a flying rock coming at me, or whatever surface awaited when I flew toward it. In recent weeks I had learned how to harness that rebounding power, and actually manipulate it. My entire plan revolved around controlling the Shield like never before.

I leaned into the wind, flapping my arms, distorting my body in any way I could until the friction of the wind flipped us over. The sight of the onrushing ocean hit my heart like a baseball bat connecting with a ball for a home run. We only had seconds.

Miyoko had not said a word since we fell, but her grip let me know that she was petrified.

"Hold on!" I yelled, realizing as I did so that it's such an instinctual thing to say, yet nothing could be more pointless to advise. A surprising calm filled me, and the magic of the First and Second Gifts took over.

I put my right arm forward, toward the rising, hungry waters, my hand balled into a fist. There was no point to this really, except that it made me feel a little more like Superman.

Sending waves of thought downward, I called upon the Ice and froze a large area of the ocean directly below us, right at the spot where we would soon impact. Mist swirled in a violent tornado and was gone in an instant, leaving a broad patch of Ice. With more thought, I hardened the area, wishing it to be the solidity of steel-enforced concrete. A tight, crackling sound met our ears as the ice compacted, shrinking into a rigid, hard foundation of cold iron.

Then Miyoko and I, bound together, hit it with the force of a small bomb.

In the milliseconds of that collision, I guided the power of the Shield with more intensity than I had ever done before. With every line of thought, with every thread of concentration, I directed the Shield in its effort to rebound us away from the harm of the rigid ice. With no time to form actual words or cohesive thoughts, I pictured in my mind the approximate direction of the flying boat and estimated its distance. All the faculties of my will exploded into the Shield, and told it what to do.

It all happened in less than a second.

When the protective bubble of the First Gift slammed into the Ice, all common sense said that the blow should have obliterated it, but it held firm, giving ammunition to the power of the Shield, making it possible for it to obey my wishes. The very air took on form. The invisible force of the protective halo surrounding us bent and twisted, a solid but unseen power. Our bodies twisted along with it, my outreached arm and fist turning to the sky, my body and Miyoko's rotating until our feet came within inches of the icy floor.

There was the briefest of pauses, like the Shield was vying for time, building its strength. The Gift's rebounding force was held in check, fostering its intensity. Then the Shield released the megaton of energy that had formed below us.

There was no fiery explosion, no streamers of heat and exhaust. There was no sound. But the Shield catapulted us into the air with the might of a thousand rockets. Miyoko screamed as we flew toward the sky, her grip tightening once again. My insides filled with a weird mixture of elation, fear, and motion sickness. I held my arm firm, straight ahead, as if I could really guide my flight.

But I knew that it was all up to physics now.

We only had to get close enough for me to shoot a stream of Ice to once again connect us with the yacht. After a few seconds of flight, a worry of doubt entered my mind that we wouldn't even come close. But then the fog of the low clouds parted, and there, directly in our path, the ship appeared.

It was like the curtain parting on a star-studded night of the Jimmy Fincher Awards Ceremony. The sight of that ship, once again within our reach, filled me with warmth and hope all over again.

But it was coming up fast, and I didn't have much time to rejoice.

Our trajectory was taking us to the left of the ship, so that we'd miss it by forty or fifty feet. Then I could see that I was being too optimistic. As the ship grew in our vision like a budding flower, it became clear that we would miss it by a great deal—too far to trust a single shot of Ice to attach us.

My mind spun in a vicious swirl of thought, assessing the situation. I concentrated on the moisture in the air up ahead of us, forming another chunk of Ice, hovering in the air, placed in a spot where I thought it was needed. We slammed into it a second after its formation, and all my mental efforts went into manipulating the reflective power of the Shield. We rebounded at the slightest of angles, still moving forward but thrown back to the right. We were now on a direct collision course with our boat.

Wet wind whipped at our faces as we approached the rear of the impossible flying object. One hundred feet became twenty. The ladder on the back sprung clearly into view. We would just miss it.

As we flew at the ladder, and then watched as it seemed to tilt in an odd angle when the direction of our flight took us past it, I focused on the bottom rung and shot a beam of Ice directly at it, incorporating the same fluidity I had learned in prior jams. The end of the rope hit home, and froze with a solid crackle around the entire area. I put a little slack into the Ice, allowing it to expand at a decelerating pace so our momentum would not rip the entire ladder from the ship.

Despite my effort, the power of our flight threw too much force into the yacht. Like tugging on a rope tied to a toy boat in the bathtub, we pulled the back of the ship in an arc, until the yacht was flying sideways, yawning dangerously toward our side. A shiver of horror went down my spine as I realized the entire ship could go tumbling end over end, tossing its occupants like a cup of dice and sending my dad from the deck to a very long fall.

A chorus of screams from the Shadow Ka showed their displeasure at this new development, and they hurried to right the ship and pull the front forward. Their uncanny ability to work in unison was as impressive as it was frightening. The ship was back to normal in a matter of seconds, just as our momentum stopped completely and we swung back toward the rear of the ship.

As we did so, I had the oddest sensation of floating in water beside the boat, watching as it seemed to rev its engines and move past us. The slack in the icy rope that attached us played out abruptly, and we shot forward, trailing the ship like tandem water skiers.

Black wings appeared from above. They were coming for their second assault.

Faster than ever before, with a flash of thought that acted before it was even formed, I shrunk the Ice, slamming us into the ladder. I wasn't going to let them cut the rope a second time. Now that we were on the ladder, I knew I could ignore the Ka and rely on the Shield to protect Miyoko and me.

I climbed up the ladder, rung by rung, freezing and unfreezing my hands to the cold, lacquered wood as we ascended. One slipped grip could send us tumbling to the ocean all over again.

Five or six Ka stayed with us, flying at us and bouncing off the Shield one after the other, screeching and clawing and taunting us. An odd thump sounded every time they hit our protective barrier, like stupid, gargantuan pigeons flying into doubled-paned windows. My confidence in the First Gift was insurmountable, but their insane actions still made me quiver, making the climb difficult. I looked down. The dark ocean lay there, a mile below us, white crested waves just visible, like faint static on television. *The storm must be picking up*, I thought, the winds stirring up the waters.

Three rungs left. Two. It felt as if Miyoko were gaining weight by the second. My back ached.

One rung. I pulled us up and over, onto the deck.

"Don't let go of me!" I yelled to Miyoko. I reached behind me and made sure my hand was squarely on her forearm, and then released the Ice that held her to me. She slumped to the ground with a heavy thump, but I kept a hold on her arm. She reached down with both arms, got her feet beneath her, and stood up.

"Okay, hold onto my arm now, and don't let go," I said.

She placed her hand around my biceps. At any other time I would have been embarrassed at how skinny my arm was, but there was no time for that right then. I swirled an icy vice around her hand, freezing her to me so I wouldn't have to worry about it. Then, I took a deep breath and looked around.

Getting up there had been the easy part. Well, not easy, but do-able. I had put so much thought and energy into that process that my head was suddenly blank of any ideas of what to do now that we were on the ship again.

But it only took five seconds for yet another brilliant Jimmy Fincher plan to pop into my head.

CHAPTER 15

One Pop at a Time

Rusty and I used to watch a show on TV about idiots. To be more specific, it was about idiots who would perform outrageous stunts and catch them on tape, as if they actually wanted to volunteer to the world just how high their level of stupidity could reach.

One of our favorites had been the one about the weather balloon guy. Weather balloons look like oversized party favors, used to send instruments into the sky in order to measure whatever it is they measure so that meteorologists can take a wild guess on whether or not it will rain. This one particular idiot decided it would be fun to attach a bunch of these helium-filled balloons to himself, until they became strong enough to lift him into the sky like something out of an old roadrunner cartoon. All he needed was a T-shirt that said "ACME" in big red letters.

His plan worked.

It worked way beyond his expectations, and soon the United States Air Force was involved, investigating something that was either a UFO or an idiot. It turned out they had found the latter.

Anyway, they came up with a method to help this guy down out of the sky without making a nasty splat on somebody's driveway, and yelled it out to him on a loudspeaker from a helicopter. (Which kept blowing the guy away with the wind from its rotating blades, giving us many opportunities to laugh uncontrollably on the floor as we watched.)

They told him to pop the balloons, one at a time, pausing after each one to see how much of a difference that one had made in keeping him in the sky. This gradual popping of the balloons worked. After popping two or three, he began to level off instead of maintaining his path toward space. Then, he popped some more and began to descend. A couple of more pops and he drifted down to the ground at a nice and comfortable speed until he was once again safe on the ground.

His elation at being alive couldn't be dampened, even as they whisked him away in a police car. I could never have known that the dumb weather balloon guy would come back to inspire me some day.

It was time to pop some Shadow Ka.

❧

They were everywhere, attached with their taut chains to the ship, wings flapping like frantic dragons. Their gray skin glistened with sweat from their exertion. I could not imagine it was easy to lift such a huge structure, no matter how many of them there were.

I knew that it was imperative to be selective in the Ka I picked off with the Ice. If too many in one area were released from the ship, it would tilt and fall to the ocean at a horrible angle. I had to keep the people inside the cabins safe, and prevent my dad from falling off the ship altogether.

Black rain spattered our faces, angry wind ripped at our clothes, frightful cries of evil filled the air.

I explained my plan to Miyoko and she looked at me with some hesitation.

"Trust me," I said, and then began the assault.

A Ka was only a few feet from us, attached to a big pipe that jutted from the deck with a railing around it, huge painted bolts dotting its surface. The Ka's chain wrapped around the pipe then up and around its neck. Its legs and arms dangled for balance as its massive wings beat at the misty air. Its ragged clothes hung like tattered laundry, flapping in the wind.

It was looking at me with black eyes as it flew, knowing it could do nothing.

With barely a thought, I sent shivers of Ice throughout the Ka's chain, freezing it until it was brittle enough to break. I formed a round ball of Ice from the air, three feet in diameter, and blasted it toward the Ka. The ball connected with the force of a catapulted stone of ancient wars, and the creature's shriek trailed off quickly as it plummeted away from the ship, toward the roiling ocean below.

The next ten minutes consisted of nothing but ice and screams. Miyoko and I walked the decks, discussing and choosing the Ka that we should blast off the ship. We tried to choose five or six that were evenly spaced around the yacht, and after they were sent in a steep, tumbling plunge to the passing ocean, the ship seemed to slow and level off. A sense of panic tingled in the air. The Ka grasped what we were doing, but there wasn't much they could do. Except release their chains and let us drop . . .

The thought made a lump form in my throat. But after the seventh Ka was ice-blasted off the ship, and it became clear to all that the remaining beasts were losing their ability to hold and carry us, they did not give up. Fighting a losing cause, the Ka beat their wings with a renewed urgency. But, just like the dope with the weather balloons, we were lightly descending to the ocean. It was actually working.

It was strange, but for the first time since the Ka had lifted the yacht, I wondered what their purpose was in kidnapping our ship. Perhaps the thought came because they did not cease their efforts in trying to fly us away even though it was obvious they could no longer succeed. Why not drop us then, letting everyone perish but me and anyone who may be lucky enough to be within touching distance? Then it hit me—thoughts of conversations I'd had with Kenji and Raspy.

The Shadow Ka knew that after the failure of the Sounding Rod, I was now indestructible. They knew that the Givers were helping me, guiding me, watching over my journey to obtain the Gifts. They could do nothing to stop me directly. Their only hope was to divert my attentions, to tempt me to abandon the Givers for other priorities. The Ka knew that if my family and friends were killed, there would no longer be even the slightest thing to hold me back from going full steam ahead in my efforts against them.

It was ironic. They wanted nothing but misery and pain for my family and me. And yet they seemed determined to keep us alive.

Collateral.

They needed the collateral against me.

It had been so when Raspy and his men took my family in America. It was so when Kenji and his thugs took my family in Japan. It was so now.

It was comforting in a very absurd way, but I also knew that it was a string that could reach its end before we knew it. I could not allow myself to ever make a judgment or assumption based on it.

I forced my thoughts back to the situation at hand.

I ran over to the railing at the edge of the yacht and looked over the side. We were getting closer to the water, perhaps halving our distance already. The ship was no longer moving forward as it descended, just straight down with a slight swaying motion, like a dry leaf falling from its limb in autumn. The remaining Ka had now put their moot efforts into simply trying to keep the boat above water.

For a fleeting moment I admired their determination. Why would they not give up? Another thought swept across my brain. Maybe I was giving them too much credit. Maybe they were just following orders and didn't think as deeply as I had assumed. It could be that they were just like the flying monkeys in *The Wizard of Oz*, dumb as dirt but very obedient. That thought brought back memories of Ole Betsy and Mayor Duck, when I really could've used some flying abilities.

A wet thump, followed by my knees buckling beneath me, announced that we had hit the water, as gentle as a drunk-piloted airplane landing. The Shadow Ka slammed into the objects they were attached to, finally giving in to defeat, and their chains loosened. They scrambled out of the metal links and folded their wings. All of the Ka, including the ones who had been flying alongside the ship, gathered together in one group, refusing to leave just yet. They came over to where Miyoko and I were standing.

One stepped forward. It was the same one who had spoken with me when they arrived the first time. His gray skin and black eyes almost blended in with the mist and rain and shadows that surrounded us. The spider web veins that covered his skin seemed to throb and pulse.

His face. It had an oriental feel to it . . . something familiar. It didn't take long for me to figure it out. Replace the splotchy hair, remove the veins, add a red bandanna . . .

I couldn't believe that I'd missed it before.

It was Kenji.

CHAPTER 16

Dad the Gift

He had changed so much in the weeks since we last met. His face was the only remaining attribute of the man I'd thought repugnant back then. Now, he was nothing but a monster—gray and hideous. He spoke first.

"You are proving to be a formidable enemy, Jimmy Fincher." He took another step closer, now just a few feet away from me. He smiled, his teeth yellow and edged in black. "We will leave for now. But know this. We are changing things in this world. A month away at sea, you have been. You will find quite a different world when you choose to return to it."

"You're always talking to me in riddles, Kenji," I said. "Just leave."

"Yes, we will leave. But, just like the first time we met, I cannot bear to depart without leaving another mystery gift. You destroyed my first, the Sounding Rod. I leave you another—one that you will not want to destroy." He leaned toward me, his hollow eyes glaring. "No, you will definitely not want to destroy this one."

Without a word, the Shadow Ka behind Kenji parted and

71

moved to the sides until a wide opening lay between two rows of the creatures. Lying there on the ground, the only sign of life his slightly moving chest, was Dad.

I looked over at Kenji. "What do you mean? What are you talking about? This is your gift to me? My dad?"

Kenji coughed—a wet, gurgled sound.

"Yes. When he awakens, you will see a horror that will far surpass anything you have yet experienced. We will see if you have the courage to do what must be done at that time."

He and the rest of the Shadow Ka unfolded their wings and took to the sky.

Fear trickled along my spine, as cold as the icy substance of my second gift. I didn't have the slightest idea what in the heck Kenji had been talking about, but it was terrifying all the same. What had they done to my dad?

I shook Miyoko from her hold on my arm, the danger gone for now, and ran over to where my dad lay, still and silent. His face was pale, his eyes closed to the whole stinking ordeal we'd just been through. A trembling apprehension filled me as I shook him, trying to get some sign that he was okay.

What had happened? What was going on in his head? What horror awaited his wakening?

I stood up and realized Miyoko was standing right next to me.

"Jimmy," she said, "this is horrible, just horrible. What is wrong with your father?"

Her voice quivered with emotion, like this was her dad,

not mine. I couldn't help but be amazed that she would feel so much for someone she hardly knew. But then I had a second thought, remembering that we'd all been together on the ship for over a month now, and had truly become an extended family. A bizarre, freak show family, but a family nonetheless.

"I don't have a clue, Miyoko." I crouched back down and touched Dad's forehead. It was warm, and his chest continued to rise and fall in a steady pattern. Again, I stood.

"He seems totally okay, like he's asleep. I can't come up with any guess at what they've done to him, although I'm worried it has something to do with that sleepy feeling we all got when they came the first time."

Miyoko noticed something and knelt down beside my dad, grabbing his arm.

"Look," she said.

She had pulled back the sleeve of his shirt, exposing his entire forearm. A small gasp escaped me.

His skin was covered with small cuts and scrapes, just healing.

"What in the—" I bent down and pulled back the sleeve on his other arm. His skin was clear on that one.

"This just keeps getting weirder," I said, and then pointed down at his arm. "Look, I bet it was done by the claws of one of the Ka. Why would they do that? Why would they possibly do that?"

Miyoko just shook her head, deep in thought.

It was at that moment that something began to bother me greatly. It was a strange silence. There was the intimidating sound of the waves of the ocean crashing against the boat, and the patter of rain on the deck, but something was missing.

Voices. I was so used to people talking and visiting and

shouting and kidding around while on the boat. I had never been on the deck and had everything so quiet. Where was everybody?

"Miyoko," I said, "what in the world is everyone doing? Why haven't they come up yet? And why didn't they try to do anything when the Ka lifted the ship? I haven't seen anyone besides Dad since this whole thing began."

A chilling worry gnawed at me, and I ran for the closest door down to the common areas.

"Stay here with my dad," I said as I opened the door.

The stairs were as dark as a cloudy eclipse.

CHAPTER 17
Human Alarm Clock

The only sounds as I descended the stairs and entered the hallway were the rapid thumps of my feet on the wood. The stillness of the air, the dark, the quiet—it was all beginning to creep me out. Something was terribly wrong.

I found the light switch and flipped it. The blast of light took me back, but a few seconds of squinting took care of it, and my eyes adjusted. I ran over to the door to the Mess Hall, and opened it. The squeaking hinges broke the silence with a grating whisper. The room was dark, and empty.

I went to my parents' room and opened the door. There was something on the bed, a long lump under the blankets. I flipped on the light. The shape did not move. I took a step closer and saw that it was my mom, lying down, her back to me.

She was fast asleep.

It didn't take a genius to understand that the odds of sleeping through a beast-powered flight in a boat were astronomical. Especially Mom. She woke up if a neighbor down the street let one fly when they rolled over in bed.

I shook her gently, with no effect. Her breathing was

heavy and regular, and she made no sign of waking up.

I ran to my room, and stumbled over Rusty on the floor. He was near the same spot I had last seen him, right after we'd seen Dad's face in the window, when I left the room to go upstairs. A quick check revealed that he was also asleep, not even having made it back to his bed.

With a heightened sense of panic, I ran throughout the rest of the ship, from room to room, even going to the crew's quarters. There was only one possibility considering what I already knew, added to the fact that no one had come up to the decks during all the commotion. So it was no surprise when I checked each room, each bed, and saw what I saw.

Everyone was in a deep sleep. From Captain Tinkles to Hood, from Joseph to the guy who made the meals (whose name always escaped me), from Rayna to Tanaka.

All of them.

They were breathing corpses.

I yelled for Miyoko, and her pounding footsteps soon announced her arrival.

"What? What is it?" she asked.

I met her in the hallway.

"Everyone is asleep, just like Dad upstairs."

"What?"

Why is it that when a person hears something that is unusual or frightening, they always ask, "What?" They hear you just fine, but feel they must ask that universal word which means, "I don't like what I just heard so maybe if I say this it will all go away and he will tell me that he was just testing to make sure my ears work and that actually everything is just fine and let's go get some dinner."

"Everyone down here is asleep," I said. "All of them, like they just can't be bothered to wake up and see what all the fuss upstairs is about." I let out a heavy sigh. "They all look just like my dad—dead to the world, but breathing. Heck, Joseph is even snoring."

Miyoko looked like it was too much to handle.

"I just don't get it," she said. "What is happening?"

I needed to act or I would go crazy.

"Come on, let's wake them up." I headed toward the Mess Hall.

"What are you going to do?" Miyoko asked.

"Get a bucket of water."

We decided to try Rusty first, because I didn't want Mom to be awake and worried about her son. We took the bucket, water slopping over the sides, and stepped into his room. I pulled and pushed on his shoulder until he finally slumped over onto his back, a small grunt escaping as he became still.

With a look at Miyoko, as if to say, "Here goes nothing," I tipped the bucket and poured its entire contents onto Rusty's face.

As it splashed down and covered his face, spreading and spilling to the floor, he looked like a diver breaking the surface after a long underwater swim. He gasped and sat up, disoriented and dazed, as if he'd been summoned from the deepest sleep of his life. Before he completely came to his senses, while still in that no man's land between sleep and waking, he said the strangest thing.

"It looks just like me! It's my face!"

Rusty stood, groggy and wet, and came back to his full senses.

"What . . . what's going on?" he asked.

"You've been asleep while I saved your hide from flying Shadow Ka," I said.

"What?" he replied (at no surprise to me).

"Come on, there's no time to explain it all right now. We've gotta wake up everybody else. You've all been sleeping, this whole time."

"But—"

"Just come on!"

We ran out into the hallway and back to the Mess Hall. Miyoko filled the bucket while I gave Rusty the shortest version possible of what had just happened.

"Those Shadow Ka came back and chained themselves to the ship and flew us into the air. They also did something weird to Dad and you guys, made you fall asleep or something. I'm worried Dad is worse, because he fell in the ocean and didn't wake up like you."

Miyoko finished filling the bucket and made for the door.

"Do you remember anything?" I continued. "What happened after I went upstairs?"

"I . . . I don't know," he said. "I kind of remember getting really tired, but it's all fuzzy. And I know I had a weird dream, but I've already forgotten it."

We went to Dad's and Mom's room first. The door was slightly ajar.

"You said something about your face when you were waking up," I said as I pushed open the door and stepped through.

"I don't remember," he said, his eyes unfocused and lost.

Mom was on the bed, the slightest hint of a snore coming from her nose. Miyoko tipped the bucket and poured about half of the water onto Mom's face. She bolted to a sitting position, spitting water.

"The Stompers!" she yelled.

Her words almost made me fall down.

"Mom! Mom! Wake up, it's me and Rusty!"

She rubbed the water out of her eyes and looked at me, then at Rusty and Miyoko.

"Was I asleep?" she asked.

"Mom," I said, "what about the Stompers? You just said something about them—did you have a dream about the Stompers? Mom?"

Dazed, she shook her head then put it in her hands, and began to sob.

I gently shook her shoulder. "Mom, talk to me."

"I had the most horrible dream, Jimmy. I . . . I can't remember anything . . . except that it was just awful."

"The Stompers, Mom, you said something about the Stompers. Try to remember."

"It's blank, completely blank."

Dejected, I turned to Rusty. "Stay with Mom; Miyoko and I will go and wake everyone else."

As we left the room, I couldn't help but feel that some major calamity was approaching.

CHAPTER 18
Dead to the World

Joseph was next in the splashed-by-water bucket brigade, followed by Rayna, Tanaka, and the members of the crew. No one else repeated any strange words or phrases when they awoke, although they had to shake away the deep slumber, and they all remembered having strange dreams.

I saved Hood for last, because I didn't feel comfortable dumping a bucket of water on his covered head. I asked Rayna if it was okay.

"Let me take care of the Hooded One," she said, and went in alone. A few minutes later, they joined us in the Mess Hall, Hood somehow looking even droopier than usual. He sat in a chair, and remained silent. Well, he was always silent, but he sat very still and offered no painted words.

I asked Joseph to go upstairs with me onto the deck of the ship and deal with Dad. I knew that somehow Dad was different—that a bucket of water wasn't going to do a thing to him. He'd been in the freezing ocean without waking up, for crying out loud. And those cuts . . .

The cuts. I stopped short just before I reached the door to

the hallway and asked everyone to show me their arms.

With raised eyebrows, everyone did as I asked, and pulled or rolled up their sleeves. Hood made a gesture to do so but hesitated, then refused.

I looked at Joseph's forearms. There were odd-looking, dangly hairs randomly placed along his arms, a couple of freckles, and even a pimple that looked like something out of a carnival freak show. But no scratches.

I examined Mom's arms next. Then Rusty. Then Tanaka, Rayna, Captain Tinkles and the other crew members. No scratches. Hood shied away when I approached him.

"Hood, what's the deal? Let me see your arm."

He shook his head, somehow showing a sense of embarrassment through the rough covering of his robe.

Rayna walked over and leaned in toward my ear.

"Jimmy," she said, "Please. You do not want . . ." She paused. "You are not ready to see the arm of the Hooded One. Please, do not push him."

Nodding, ignoring the intense curiosity that sprung up in my head, I looked at Hood and tried to appear patient and understanding.

"Well," I said, "What about your arms, Hood? Do they have scratches on them?"

He shook his head. He was okay in that regard, but I just couldn't help wondering what was up with this guy. I thought about the time we found him deep in the woods after we'd been to the Pointing Finger, and I had seen him in the distance—robeless, eerily pale, and hunched. Rayna and Miyoko had told me to wait while they went to him and clothed him once again in his robe. Raspy had stolen it to fool us into leading him to the Givers' book.

Rayna had said something similar then, something about how I should not see him yet. I knew he had other clothes on beneath the robe, so it wasn't like they were protecting his modesty. Was it his identity, his true identity they were trying to conceal? Could he perhaps be someone that I had known earlier in my life? I made a note in my head to grill Rayna or Miyoko about it later.

"Jimmy-san," Tanaka asked, "why you go crazy and ask to see our arms?"

"I'm not crazy, Tanaka." I pointed upward, indicating the place where my dad lay. "Dad is up there, sleeping like a dead man, and he's been dragged through cold water and dropped and flown through the air, and he's showing no signs of waking up. I think something is wrong with him, more than the weirdness of you guys all sleeping like you were. Anyway, he has small cuts all over his right forearm."

"Small cuts?" Rayna said. "On one arm only?"

I thought for a second to make sure. "Yeah, just the right one. Does that mean anything?"

She shook her head.

"Jimmy," Joseph said, "what in the world were you talking about, saying your dad had been dragged through water and all that? What happened up there?"

"Come on, I'll tell you up there. Miyoko, why don't you stay down here and tell these guys what happened, too."

"All right," she said. "I just hope they believe me."

"Are you serious? How could anything surprise us anymore?" I grabbed Joseph's arm. "Let's go."

After everything that had happened so far that day, I half-expected Dad to be gone when we walked out onto the deck. But he was there, on his back, motionless, like a fallen soldier left for the vultures. It surprised me how relieved I felt when we could see that his chest still rose and fell with regularity. Obviously, my confidence that he was okay was weakening.

"My goodness," Joseph said, then ran to his side.

He grabbed Dad's cheeks and pinched them, then lightly slapped them. "Come on, old boy, wake up! J.M.! Wake up, man! Can you hear me?"

Frustrated, Joseph gently laid Dad's head back down and let go.

"Jimmy, what have we gotten ourselves into?" He looked at me, pain in his eyes.

"I don't know," I said, barely above a whisper. For the first time that day, I wanted to fall down and bawl my eyes out.

"We should try the water on him, too," Joseph said. "I'll go get it."

As he left and went down into the cabin area, I picked up Dad's arm and looked at the scratches again. With more time to look, I realized that I had missed something earlier. The cuts were not quite as random as I had thought. There was something . . . regular about them. They didn't quite form a word, but there was some definite shape or reason to their arrangement—almost like a string of several letter 'O's intertwined. Something lingered on the edges of my mind, like trying to remember the name of a friend from an old neighborhood—it was somewhere in the old memory bank, but just didn't feel like coming out yet.

The scratches meant something. What was it? It was beginning to drive me bonkers.

Joseph ran up behind me, water sloshing out of the bucket as he came, making hard splattering sounds, like a drunk and his spittoon in an old western.

"Watch out," he said.

I stood back and watched as Joseph poured the water onto Dad's face.

Nothing. Not a flinch or a twitch. The only movement was the hair on his head and eyebrows as the cold water washed over him.

Joseph knelt down again, ignoring the wetness of the deck, and brought his ear down until it hovered just above Dad's nose and mouth. Joseph's eyes were looking in my direction, and then he closed them, concentrating.

"I can definitely hear him breathing, although it seems so faint and shallow." He brought his head back up and looked down at Dad. "I hate to do this, but let's try one more thing."

Joseph put his hand on Dad's arm, grabbed some skin, and pinched it with all of his might. No response.

Something was seriously wrong with my father.

CHAPTER 19

Tanaka Gets Freaky

That night we all sat around the table, miserable in our attempt to be normal. We'd put Dad in his bed, and he lay there now, covered and silent. His breathing continued to be normal, but he would not respond in any way to our efforts to wake him. We'd finally given up.

Miyoko had done a great job of catching up everyone on our adventures in the ocean and in the air. It seemed impossible that they could have slept through the whole thing, but no one remembered much at all. Only Rusty recalled anything relating to the attack—the haunted vision of Dad's face in the window.

"What do we do?" asked Rayna. "Perhaps we should head for land, get a doctor for your father."

"Yes," Tanaka said. "Yes. We go now, get doctor for your papa." He stood up from his chair and walked over to me. "Jimmy-san. You, me, we become best friends, neh?"

I nodded, but couldn't say anything. He continued.

"What is dear to you is dear to me. If I, if Tanaka-san," he put his hand on his chest, "could replace himself with your papa, I would do it. I swear to the *okisaru* I would do it."

"Thank you, Tanaka. I mean it. Thanks."

Tanaka's face changed a bit, his eyes looking beyond me, a look of confused contemplation washing over him. He stared, unmoving.

"Tanaka?" I said, worried the old man had finally gone over the edge.

He blinked, shook his head, and ran his fingers through his greasy hair. He pulled at his eyebrows, scratched his nose. His eyes focused once again on mine, but he said nothing.

"Tanaka?" I asked again. "What's wrong with you?"

"Uh . . . uh. Wrong? No . . . no, nothing is wrong, my friend." He slowly shook his head back and forth as he stumbled back to his chair and plopped down into it.

Miyoko got up and ran to him, kneeling down and putting her hand on his knee.

"Father, what is wrong?"

Tanaka still had a dazed look, his forehead wrinkled and eyes squinted as he continued to ponder whatever thoughts had overtaken him as he spoke to me.

"I . . . don't know what to say. When I mentioned the *okisaru*, something . . ."

He patted Miyoko on the shoulder, then stood and headed for the door.

"I am sorry, my friends. I must rest."

He left the room without another word. Miyoko followed him.

"What in the heck just happened?" Rusty asked.

I then told the story of the *okisaru* to those who had not been there—about the giant monkey we'd met while searching for Hood weeks ago.

"And that's all I can really tell you," I said after relating the details. "I don't understand it any better than you do. A huge monkey reached over, touched Tanaka in the forehead, then vanished into the trees. That's it."

"And you say these *okisaru* are some kind of ancient legend?" Joseph asked.

"Yeah, I guess. Tanaka said something about them being wise and powerful or something. But after it touched him on the forehead, Tanaka didn't say a word. Not a word."

Everyone was silent for a while, trying to picture a ten-foot-tall monkey.

"This is too much for me; I'm going to sit with your dad," Mom said. I could tell she was on the edge of losing her composure, tears welling up in her eyes.

"Okay, Mom," I said.

"You guys figure out what we're going to do," she said as she walked to the open door. "I . . . think it would be best to find a doctor. But I also know that Jimmy has important things to accomplish."

She walked back to me and put her hand on my head, lightly tousling my hair.

"Jimmy, ultimately this is your decision. I promise I'll support whatever it is you decide."

"Mom, don't talk like that. You're scaring me."

"I'm serious, Jimmy." She knelt down beside me, looking into my eyes. "Listen to me. We all know the heavy burden that is on your shoulders. Dad would not want you to put that to the side for him." A tear trickled down her cheek. "Deep inside of me I know that we must continue on and find the Third Gift."

She stood, and tried to smile. "I'll be with Dad." She hurried out of the room before the tears really started to flow.

It was now me, Rayna, Hood, and Joseph.

"What do we do?" I asked them.

"Your mom is right, Jimmy," Joseph said. "It's your choice. Although I must admit it's a little strange to take orders from a guy for whom I used to change stinky diapers."

I winced. "Please, Joseph, don't conjure up that image in my head. All I need is a picture of you handling a wet-wipe."

"I think we should do what we decided before your father became ill," Rayna said.

Joseph and I looked at her.

"You mean the IDL?" Joseph asked. "Head for the International Date Line, follow it across half the world until we find some tower that may not even exist, leaving Jimmy's father in bed, perhaps dying of some otherworldly disease? Do all of this on some bizarre notion I got while reading a note we found in a bottle in the middle of the ocean that is forty years old? This is what you think we should do?"

Rayna nodded, calm and collected.

"I agree," Joseph said with a smile.

They looked at me.

I knew that what I said next was of such importance that, no matter how cliché or ridiculous it sounded, could forever change the course of our lives and the entire world. I had no misgivings or naïve hopes about my dad and what we could do for him. The odds of a normal doctor helping him were slim, even if we could possibly spare the time to find one.

That was the problem. There was just no time. In the span of one month, we'd seen the Shadow Ka go from mostly human to mostly not human. Things were in fast forward, happening way quicker than I ever would've thought back when I blocked the Black Curtain.

For all we knew, the Curtain was no longer blocked at all. And Mom was right about what Dad would want us to do. We had no choice, really, so making one was much easier than it seemed.

I stood up.

"Let's do this thing," I said, slapping Joseph on the side of his bald, shiny head. "We're heading for the IDL."

CHAPTER 20

Not Photogenic

Our journey took weeks.

If I hated the ocean before, it now became something that ate at my insides like a sickness. I longed for the sight of land so much that I had to force myself not to think about it. It got to the point where I felt like I was hypnotizing myself, almost pretending that I was inside a cartoon or virtual reality world—convincing myself that we were not actually surrounded by endless miles of nothing but blue-green water.

I don't know how good ole Christopher Columbus could stand it.

Dad continued to sleep, quiet in his coma.

Mom figured out how to feed him, although it took a good hour to do it every time. Her patience was astounding, as she forced his body to take on reflexes that even sleep could not ignore. It was a messy, tiring process. But Mom did not complain, and Dad continued to live.

The scratches on Dad's arm healed, leaving obvious scars that continued to nag at my brain, trying to pull some memory or thought out of its dark recesses. I knew that the pattern of the slightly raised scar tissue meant something, but it eluded me every time I sat and strained my thoughts trying to figure it out.

Boredom was the only thing worse than the ocean. Or maybe it was the boredom itself that made me despise the ocean. Either way, we were reaching the very edge of our tolerances. I think we were all about to go insane.

There's not much of those days that is worth recalling.

But there were two occurrences that would end up meaning very much indeed.

And despite the weeks and weeks of travel, in one of those quirky things of life, both things happened on the same day.

It was late, and the others had gone to sleep. Rayna was in the Mess Hall with me, both of us eating a light snack, tired but with no desire to sleep. There'd been something I had wanted to ask Rayna for quite some time, so I decided to lead up to it by making some conversation about other things first.

"How can this ship possibly have so much food?" I asked after a few minutes of silence.

"I don't know, it's very big," Rayna said, studying her yogurt. "It's made for twenty times our number, so it has plenty of food." She looked up at me. "I guess I've never really thought about it."

"It seems like the food would go bad or something." I yawned. "But I ain't complaining, trust me."

There were another few moments of silence.

"It's also weird how Joseph got the money to afford this boat," I said. "I know for a fact that bald-headed monkey is not rich. And I remember he said something about it making sense some day. I'd kind of forgotten about that until now."

"You worry about it too much, Jimmy. Eat your chips."

After a few more minutes of meaningless talk about the weather getting warmer and warmer as we headed south along the IDL, I asked the question.

"Rayna, will you look at a picture for me?"

She eyeballed me with a look of certain disapproval. She knew what I meant.

"You know. With your gift."

I pulled out a picture my mom had, a five-by-ten of me in fifth grade. I pushed it over to Rayna.

"Jimmy, you know this is not something I use lightly."

"Please, Rayna. I need something, something that can give me hope. Please?"

"Knowing your future is not a good thing. What if you see yourself being killed tomorrow? What would you do?"

Her question gave me shivers. "I . . ."

"Jimmy, I use my gift for assistance, to guide us when it is possible. I do not use it for cheap fortune telling."

"Okay, then. How about a compromise?"

"What is it?" she asked, hinting that she did not like my tone.

"Well, you are the only one who can truly manipulate a picture into telling the absolute, for-sure future. But when you have touched it with your gift, others can see . . . you know . . . alternate *possibilities* of the future. Right?"

She nodded, still making sure I knew she disapproved of where I was leading her.

"If I could just see different versions of the future, and if just one of those was something good and positive, it would give me hope. Right now, the last few days . . . I feel like giving up, that we are chasing an impossible thing. Will you please do this for me?"

"No," she said, rather curtly.

"Then why did you do it to those pictures that Hood had, when I first met him?"

"I did not give the Hooded One permission to take those pictures."

"Oh, come on, Rayna! Please?" Then, I resorted to that last desperate plea of a kid, which I still was, although sometimes I had to remind myself of that fact. "Pretty please?" I said.

She stared at me, thinking. A minute passed. Just as I was about to make my final request before giving up, Rayna picked up the picture.

"Leave for five minutes, then come back. I will let you look at it for one minute. Then, we tear it up and throw it overboard."

"But—"

All she did was raise her eyebrows, and I knew I was pushing my luck.

"Okay," I said. I left the Mess Hall and went up onto the deck to wait it out.

I thought it would be the longest five minutes of my life, until I saw Tanaka on the deck of the ship.

I'd completely forgotten that Tanaka was taking his turn at watch, sitting alone on a lawn chair, searching the skies for winged gray people.

"Ah, Jimmy-san! You come to visit me, neh? I told you—I

will not tuck you in any more! Go back to bed." His unearthly roar of a laugh pierced the air, and I was glad, for at least a brief moment, that there was no one within hundreds of miles to hear it.

"You are such a comedian, Tanaka."

Almost everything I said to him was sarcastic, but I loved that guy like a favorite uncle. He had returned to his normal self after the strange night when the mention of the *okisaru* had unsettled him so much. And he would not speak of it, either.

"So," I said, "anything interesting out here?"

"No, not much to talk about, I'm glad to say. Why are you awake, my friend?"

"Can't sleep. Rayna and I are just shooting the breeze down there, eating junk food. Well, I was eating junk—Rayna was eating yogurt."

"Yogurt? Yogurt! That stuff is like eating melted feet!"

He got me. Despite everything, I laughed out loud for several seconds.

"Good one," I said after bringing myself under control.

After that we were silent for a moment. The night air was moist, and the ocean was still, the only sound the soft lapping of the water against the side of the boat. Sure that five minutes had passed, I was anxious to get back to Rayna and headed toward the door that led downstairs.

"Gee, thanks for long visit," said Tanaka.

"Sorry, I told Rayna I'd only be a minute. I . . . just wanted to say hi to you, that's all. See ya."

"Yes, my boy. Good night. If big flying monsters come, I'll let you know, neh?"

"Yeah, sounds good."

I headed downstairs to see my future.

Rayna sat at the table, her hands folded and resting on top of my picture. She did not look at me when I walked into the room.

"Did you do it?" I asked.

"Yes, I did." She rose, and walked toward the door. "If I were you, I would not look at it. Nothing good will come of it. If you see something hopeful, you will fear that it may never happen. If you see something dreadful, you will fear that it will. There is nothing to gain from this."

"What did you see?"

"Once its magic began, I looked away. I do not wish to see your future, Jimmy. The choice is yours to make, but I would not." She narrowed her eyes and brought up a finger. "But please remember. If you do look at it, nothing is certain. I can sometimes see the absolute future with enough effort, but what you will see are only possibilities. Do you understand?"

I nodded.

"Good night. If you see something frightful, please don't come crying to me. Let your mother console you."

And with that, she left, closing the door behind her.

The entire time she'd spoken, I'd kept a solemn face, trying to convey the feeling that I was considering her words with great care, contemplating what I should do. But I knew all the while that I was going to look at the picture. How could I not?

I walked around the table and sat in the chair beside the photograph. I purposefully averted my eyes until I was ready to look. After taking a deep breath, I pulled the photo over until it was right in front of me, just inches away from my eyes. And then, with a thousand pounds of TNT exploding in my chest, I looked.

I stared at the photo for ten to fifteen minutes.

Only two images appeared.

In both of them, I was dead.

CHAPTER 21

Undesirable Choices

The first image was one I had seen before, although very briefly, in the house by the river in Japan, where I first met the Hooded One. Countless pictures had been hung on the walls, Hood's strange way of welcoming me to that house that Rayna had foreseen being near the place I fell into the river. Rayna had touched each of those pictures with her gift, and I saw a particular image in each one of them.

I saw the same thing in this new picture on the table.

It was me, dead, or at best, in a deep sleep, lying on a bed of stone, with nothing but gray surrounding my body. My skin was pale and lifeless. It reminded me of an ancient photograph, in black and white, of a dead soldier from the Civil War I had once seen in a history textbook. It sent shivers from head to toe, and I closed my eyes once or twice, squeezing them tight, hoping that the picture would soon change into something else, something more positive.

About the third time I did this, a new image awaited when I opened my eyes.

This one was even stranger, although no less frightening.

The view was from thirty or forty feet above the ground, looking down on a large, coffin-shaped enclosure of clear glass. Within the glass structure was a soft bed with a person on top of it, asleep or dead. The person was me, looking just as blank and pale as in the other image. I wore a dark suit, and didn't look much older at all.

For a few seconds I could do nothing but stare at myself, almost expecting to see movement—an eye twitch, a yawn, rolling over onto my side. But of course, it was a photo, and nothing moved. Then I noticed everything else in the picture.

Completely surrounding the glass encasement were a group of soldiers, standing at the ready, machine guns raised in defense. They were dressed in green military issue, but with no distinctive flags or emblems proclaiming whom they represented. The soldiers and the glass wherein I was laying all sat atop a rectangular pyramid of steps, at least fifty feet high. The bottom-most step was surrounded in barbed wire and heavy fencing material.

Outside of this barrier were people—lots of people—going all the way to the very edge of the picture. They were just standing there, looking upward at the soldiers and me. Some of them were holding flowers and ribbons.

It made no sense, but it put a lump in my heart.

After a minute or two, the picture faded back into its original form—my school picture. I waited for something to change again, but nothing happened.

The heavy feeling of dread that filled me was almost unbearable. What did it mean? Were those two pictures the only possible future before me? Surely there was something else, some far better outlook. Despite the heavy, vile feeling inside of me, I could not truly believe that no matter what I did, I would end up dead—be it in a world of gray dreariness or camped inside some glass coffin.

There had to be something else. There had to be.

Perhaps it was all a vain wish, a way for my brain and heart to deceive me so that I would continue on in the fight. But I surprised even myself when I stood up and threw the picture into the trash can. A renewed sense of determination filled me. I would not let some dumb photograph ruin my life or make me give up.

I convinced myself that the picture had just neglected to show all the possibilities. I would avoid both of them, and we would somehow win this bizarre battle against an unknown and so far unseen enemy called the Stompers. I wasn't sure where it came from, but I was filled with strength, and decided to go chat with Tanaka until I felt tired.

I went upstairs and found him snoring loud enough to wake the fish at the bottom of the ocean.

I woke Tanaka up and reminded him of his important duty as watch guard, and then went to my room, just as Rayna was sneaking back into the Mess Hall and retrieving the picture I'd left behind. She would not tell me about it for a very long time to come, but the photo had transformed into a third prophetic image—one that was even worse than the two I had seen.

CHAPTER 22

Another Dream

❦

I am standing in a field of grass, the most brilliant green I have ever seen, like thin slivers of emerald reaching for the heavens. The sky is radiant and blue above me, unbroken by even the slightest wisp of cloud. The air is warm and still. There is no sound.

I look around, and what I find is very surprising to me.

To my left, about fifty yards away, there is a wooden chair, just like the ones my family has around our kitchen table. Sitting in the chair is Mom, hands in her lap, looking in my direction with a big smile on her face. I begin to wave but then I see that her eyes are not focused on me, but on something in the distance.

I look in that direction, behind me.

There is another chair, just like Mom's, about the same distance from me. Dad is sitting in this one, looking over at Mom, the same smile on his face. Their smiles do not comfort me, they scare me—there is something not right about them, like the clowns at a cheap carnival. It's creepy.

I call to both of them but they do not answer.

Then their expressions change from eerie cheer to utter horror. They look up to the sky. I follow their gaze.

Two balls of fire are hurtling from the sky, trails of flame marking their path. It doesn't take long to realize they are heading for my mom and dad, both on a direct course to obliterate them in a fiery instant of brief pain.

I yell for them to run, but it's as if I'm not there. They ignore me, they ignore their own instincts, they ignore each other. They just sit and wait for certain death.

A splinter of panic pierces my heart. The meteors are moving too fast—there is no way I can get to them both in time. I know that I can save them with the power of the Shield, but I need more time.

The burning rocks are coming, coming faster. They will be here in seconds. What do I do? I am safe because of the Shield, but my parents are not. I can save them if they would only help by running to me.

I yell again, urging them to run. They do not hear, or they choose not to.

I realize I must choose. I can still save one of them. I must choose.

I can't. My feet stay planted on the ground as if caught in invisible glue. My conscience will not allow me to choose between my parents. It is a choice that doesn't register properly in the brain—it is something that a child cannot, and should not, deal with.

So I do nothing.

The plummeting rocks of angry inferno are only feet above my parents, the moment of impact milliseconds away.

Too late, I remember my second Gift. The Ice. Could it have stopped the meteors?

My wail of pain and guilt is swallowed by the thunderous noise of twin explosions.

For the third time since my strange story began, I awoke from my sleep in a pool of sweat, the horrors of a dream lingering in the air like haunted mist. This one was even more real than the others. Why? Why was I having these dreams? I didn't remember ever having nightmares before in my life.

The stress. Maybe that's what it was. Going through such terrifying experiences did whacked-out things to the brain, and these dreams could have been a result.

Still breathing heavily, I tried to go back to sleep. It would take awhile, but eventually I drifted off, this time without nightmares.

It was odd that the dream and the picture incident with Rayna occurred on the same day, sandwiched between so many uneventful weeks. But other than those two things, there wasn't much worth noting or remembering. The days dragged, and the nights were dark and sad.

Dad remained in his coma, Mom at his side constantly. The Shadow Ka didn't bother us, and the night watches got to the point where we didn't take them seriously anymore. But we continued them, just in case.

The ocean had become my home, and I couldn't remember or imagine life without it. The storms, the waves, the rain, the smell, the sounds—it had all become a part of me. Keeping the cabin fever and insanity at bay was becoming more and more difficult, but we did everything we could think of to keep our minds and our bodies exercised. We played games, we vigorously cleaned the ship, we jogged in circles and did pushups and sit-ups, we taught each other things we'd learned in our different stages of life—we tried to keep busy.

It wasn't all bad. Some days were more fun than others. My favorite memories were the soft golden glow of sunsets, sending hues of orange and red across the cloudy sky, and the camaraderie of our group, both family and friends. They made it bearable.

But any way you look at it, there was no doubt that the seventieth day since we left Japan was one that brought a great deal of relief. It brought change, and change was what we needed more than anything else to stave off the madness and the monotony.

That was the day we saw the huge gaping hole in the ocean.

CHAPTER 23

The Abyss

It was one of those sights that your brain has a difficult time accepting. What we saw in the water before us was impossible. And yet, with several sets of eyes serving as witnesses, it was undeniably real.

We were fortunate to come upon the anomaly during the day, when Captain Tinkles could see it in plenty of time to stop the ship from running into it. It was his cry of alarm over the loudspeakers that brought us all up to the front of the yacht to look out upon the hole in the water. And although it made no sense until later, that's exactly what it was.

A hole. An emptiness. An *abyss* in the water.

The captain pulled up about fifty feet short from the edge of the hole. A sharp and defined point of the hole was closest to the ship, and then it stretched out like a "V" away from us for thirty or forty feet, until both sides turned sharply and came back together again, forming a perfect square, although it looked like a diamond from our vantage point.

The water abruptly ended along each edge of the square,

actually lapping against some unseen force, then plummeted downward in perfectly flat walls of water.

It looked like someone had taken a massive, square-shaped tube of glass and placed it into the water, reaching all the way to the bottom of the ocean. The top of the glass would have risen well above the surface, because the waves in the water did not go cascading over the edges of the abyss, but repelled backward, just as if they were hitting a stone wall.

If it was a glass building in the middle of nowhere, it was the cleanest in history, because we could not see any reflections or dirt. It looked for all the world like there was an invisible force-field holding back the water, just like in some old science fiction movie.

"What could that possibly be?" asked Joseph.

For several minutes we stared, craning our necks for a better view. The urge to peek over the edge and see how far down the thing went was nearly unbearable.

I turned to Captain Tinkles. "Is that thing on the IDL?"

"Yes it is," he said. "According to my instruments it straddles the imaginary line right down the middle. And nothing in my records indicates anything should be here."

I don't know for sure what it was we were expecting, but that big hole had to be it. This had to be the Tower of Air. I said as much to the others.

"You think that's the Tower?" asked Joseph. "It sure doesn't look like a tower to me. It looks like a big hole into another dimension or something. It's flat out freaky is what it is."

"Think about it. We're looking for something on the International Date Line. That's where we are." I pointed toward the abyss. "This just happens to be something that defies any logic or sense from our own world. Do you really think it's a coincidence? This has to be it."

"Remember what it's called," said Rayna. "The Tower of Air."

We said nothing, waiting for her to go on.

"Well," she said, "maybe that's exactly what this thing is—a tower of air. Maybe it's air pushing against the water, holding it back, like the world's biggest wind tunnel or something. I don't know, but I'm with Jimmy on this one—it has to be the Tower of Air."

No one argued.

"Well, let's go check it out," said Joseph.

"Captain Tinkles," I said, walking up to him. "Do you have a raft or something that a couple of us could take closer to the hole, so that we don't have to worry about endangering the yacht?"

"Yes, yes, we do, of course we do. I'll go and prepare it."

I turned toward the others.

"All right, who's coming with me?"

Everyone wanted to go. But I insisted that it wasn't the smart thing to do, just in case something crazy happened. I told them that I was going for sure, and that two more could come with me. Everyone else had to stay on the yacht.

"Well, I'm definitely going," said Joseph. "So the rest of you will have to fight it out."

"I'm going as well." This was Rayna.

A chorus of arguments sprang up, everyone throwing out reasons why they in particular should go.

"Hold it!" I yelled. "Come on, guys, if it's something really cool, you can all take turns going to see it." I walked over to Rusty, and put my hand on his shoulder. "You stay here with Mom—I don't think we should leave her alone in case Dad wakes up or something and she needs help."

This brought complaints from not just Rusty, but Mom, too. Everyone started arguing again.

"Fine," I said. "I'll decide. Joseph and Rayna are coming with me. If everything is safe, we'll take others to see it later. Now, let's go."

Rusty punched me in the arm. "I think you forget that I'm your big brother, Jimmy."

Wondering why the Shield didn't stop him, then figuring it was because I deserved it, I said, "And I think you forget that I'm the one with the Shield and Ice, and you better be nice to me."

"All right, you two," Mom said. "Stop your bickering, and let's get on with it." She came up to me and gave me her off-to-school hug. "Please be careful, son. I don't want to have to take care of you and Dad both."

"I will, Mom. Rusty, I promise I'll take you out to see it later."

"Whatever," he said, and sulked off toward the cabins.

Although I would not say it out loud, I made Rusty stay because I didn't want to take a chance of anything bad happening to him. I could only hope he'd understand eventually.

With a heavy hurt in my gut, I motioned to Joseph and Rayna, and we headed for the raft.

CHAPTER 24

Rafting

Nothing in my experience has ever matched the sheer intimidation of being in a small rubber raft in the middle of the ocean. It felt so odd, like we would be swallowed at any minute by the deep blue waters. It took several minutes before I could settle myself and calm down. I thought that perhaps my experience in saving Dad from drowning had created a phobia of water.

Rayna and Joseph told me to sit up front while they used the wooden paddles provided by Captain Tinkles to row us toward the gaping abyss. The water was relatively calm, but the boat bobbed up and down with the great waves that were so large it was impossible to distinguish or mark them. My stomach was already beginning to turn, and I felt sad that if I did throw up, Tanaka would not be around to catch it for me.

We didn't speak as we approached the invisible retaining wall; instead, we kept our eyes peeled for any indication of what it was we had discovered. A seething fear was growing inside me that some malicious beast would fly out of the depths of the hole and have us for supper.

As we got closer, I could better make out the details of the anomaly. The two edges closest to us were sharply defined, ending abruptly against the barrier—the water really did appear to be sloshing up against a glass wall. Looking to the far side at the other two walls of the square hole, we could see the opposite perspective. Where the water hit the force-field, it flattened completely, then descended in a plane until it went beyond our field of vision. We were witnessing the largest aquarium in the world, and I couldn't help but wonder at how much money we could make off such a spectacular display.

We came to within two feet, then stopped.

"Reach out," Joseph said. "See if there really is a wall there."

A nervous tension ran up my spine, like I was approaching the very edge of the roof on a seventy-floor building. My heart was beating in small, rapid explosions. My hands were sweaty and my eyes were watery. I had to squeeze them shut a time or two to clear my vision.

I grasped a seam on the edge of the raft with a firm hold, then leaned out over the water toward the invisible wall. I held my other hand out, palm flat and facing forward, until it was just an inch or two in front of where the wall should be. Before I went further, I looked down, and almost fainted when I saw the descending walls of water ending in blackness far below. I shuddered, and looked back up at my hand.

With exaggerated care, I moved my hand forward.

It bumped into something invisible, but nothing like I would have expected—it rebounded, just slightly. It was solid, but soft, like touching a balloon that was filled to capacity with helium. I pushed again, this time a little harder, and it burst through the barrier. I gasped and had to catch myself with my legs and other hand or I would've fallen out of the raft.

A tickling sensation surrounded my wrist in a perfect ring, in the exact spot where the barrier wall would be. I pulled my hand back out with no difficulty, then bounced it a couple of more times on the force field. I pulled back and sat down in the boat.

"Man, that was weird," I said.

"Let me try," Rayna said. She crawled over to the other side of the raft and stuck her hand out. It rebounded just a little like mine did, then she pushed her hand through, and wiggled her fingers on the other side. After a few seconds, she pulled it back and returned to her rowing position.

"Joseph, you do it," she said. "That way we'll all know what we're dealing with."

Joseph did as he was told, trying to act like he was obliging her when it was obvious he was dying to see what it felt like. When he'd finished, he had a huge grin on his face.

"That is some kind of bizarre," he said. "I don't think there's any doubt that this is it, friends. This is definitely the Tower of Air."

"What makes you so sure?" I asked.

"Well, didn't you feel it? I think that's air that is repelling the water. Not some magic force field or invisible wall—I think it's just air. I don't know how in the world it works, but it's air. That's why it holds the water back, but with enough of a push you can go right through it." He let out a huge sigh. "These Givers never cease to amaze, do they?"

"Okay," I said, "I'll agree that this is the Tower of Air. But what do we do now? I mean, yeah, it's cool and all that, but how is it supposed to help me get the Third Gift? I don't think I'm quite ready to squeeze through the barrier of air and fall to my death at the bottom of the—"

Something caught my vision, cutting me short.

"What?" asked Rayna.

"What is that over there?" I said in reply.

On the opposite wall from where we were currently bobbing in the water, there was an odd protrusion on the inside of the tower, jutting out from the wall of flat water toward us. It was impossible to tell exactly what it was, but it appeared regular and consistent in size. It started at the very top, near the surface where the water was breaking against the wall of air, and descended at an angle down into the depths of the tower, zigzagging back and forth until I lost sight of it, the wall on our side clipping it from my view.

"Holy camoli," I said, barely a whisper.

"What?" Joseph and Rayna said at the same time, snapping me out of my dazed stare.

"I think those are stairs over there."

CHAPTER 25

The Edge of Water

We rowed the raft around the square Tower until we reached the other side. The only sound was the splash and swish as the paddles entered the water and pulled us along. We were too focused on the stairs, watching as they became clearer.

They were made out of water.

At least, that's what it looked like. Their color and consistency were exactly the same as the inner walls of the tower, meaning the force of the magic air was repelling and shaping the water into steps. Just as the walls looked like a huge aquarium, the stairs looked like they were made out of glass—an extension of the aquarium walls.

I began to itch with excitement to try those steps and see what waited at the bottom. My earlier feelings of nausea, fear, and intimidation were fading, replaced by intense anticipation. I knew this was the Tower of Air, the place that old Farmer had told me held the Third Gift. The feeling inside of me was like Christmas morning times ten.

I just couldn't wait to see what the Gift would be,

although I was a little nervous considering the riddle I'd had to solve to get the Second Gift.

As we rounded the final corner of the tower, the stairs slipped out of sight, obscured now by the edges of water. Joseph and Rayna did their best to guess where the topmost stair had been, and took the raft there. We approached the edge of the abyss, and it was difficult to ignore the frightening feeling the image brought to us, like those last seconds must feel before one goes over the Falls of Niagara.

An unexpected wave pushed us into the wall of air. We bounced off just as if we'd hit a dock or a wall. It was so strange, our eyes refusing to believe what we were seeing. It looked like we should have toppled over the edge like a daredevil in a wooden barrel, but it didn't happen.

"Okay," Joseph said, "although I certainly didn't mean to do that, at least now we know we're safe going along the edge. Jimmy, stick your head through the wall of air and see if you can spot the stairs."

I braced my hands on the raft and went for it. I put my head against the invisible barrier, and rubbed my hair against it. It gave a little, but I didn't pop through. Again, it was like rubbing my head against a giant balloon. I stopped, then more firmly pushed the top of my head against the wall. It slipped through—once it started it was as smooth as putting your head through the waterfall at one of those amusement parks. The tingling sensation that represented the actual substance of the wall tickled as it went down my face before settling on my neck.

I looked around.

"Just a few more feet that way," I said, pointing to my right.

I pulled my head out, and Rayna and Joseph rowed the boat to the spot I indicated. I poked through the wall of air again, and saw that we were directly over the first step. The stairs of repelled water led down to the right, then hit a landing where it jutted out from the wall further so that more stairs could zigzag back the other way. I wondered how deep the thing went.

I popped out and told them I was ready to go. "One of you needs to stay with the raft, and I don't feel like another argument on who gets to go with me."

Joseph and Rayna looked at each other.

"How about rock, paper, scissors?" Joseph asked.

Rayna let out a little laugh, then agreed.

Joseph won.

"That's fine," Rayna said. "But if something terrible happens, if you're not back in an hour or so, I'm coming after you."

"Sounds like a plan," I said. The others waiting on the yacht were yelling at us, wondering what was going on. Joseph told them we had found stairs and were going to explore the tower. I couldn't imagine how anxious they felt having to watch from a distance.

I sat on the edge of the raft, with Joseph supporting me from behind, and pushed both feet into the wall of air. They popped through and I felt them come down to rest on the top step. It wiggled slightly when I touched it.

"Okay, push me through."

Joseph gave me a strong nudge and the rest of my body slid through the tower wall, the tingling sensation sweeping across my body until I was completely inside. The top landing where the stairs began was about five feet by five feet, and I was standing in the middle of it. The wiggling continued, like I'd just stepped onto a firm water bed, but it held.

I knelt down closer to the floor of water, and put my hand on it, palm flat. The sensation was different from this side— there was no feeling of a rubber balloon. It had the firm feel of a wall, but felt very wet, just as it would if you touched normal water. I brought my hand away and it was indeed soaking wet. So were the bottoms of my shoes.

Joseph's feet came through and almost knocked me on the head, and then his body followed. I couldn't help but wonder what the Shield would have done if he had hit me with his foot.

"Wow," Joseph said. "This is unbelievable. I just can't. . . this is amazing!"

"Touch the water," I said.

Joseph knelt down and did so, then stood and looked at his wet hand.

"This has got to be one of the weirdest things I've ever experienced, and don't forget, I've been through some crazy stuff in the Blackness."

We now had a perfect view of the Tower of Air's interior, and it was awesome. It now had much more of a feeling of being inside a building, a true tower. The repelled walls of water shot downward in four flat planes, going from a brilliant, sparkling blue at the top to a dark, lightless color toward the bottom.

Looking down, it reminded me of a drawing I had done for my mom when I was in first or second grade. I had been sketching a tunnel, and I'd done it by connecting straight lines from each corner of the page to the corners of a small square in the middle of the page. That's what it looked like, peering over the edge of the stairs toward the bottom of the enormous tower.

Joseph had his backpack, and I was glad we'd remembered to bring flashlights, because it looked like we would need them when we reached the bottom. It was going to be quite a trip by the looks of it.

"Shall we?" asked Joseph.

"Let's do it."

I turned and waved at Rayna.

"Please be careful," she said. "I will come after you if I don't see you soon."

Her words took me back, because for some reason I thought we wouldn't be able to talk through the walls of air. But there was no muffling or distortion of her words, and she had obviously heard our entire conversation so far.

"Whoa," I said. "I don't know why, really, but I thought I wouldn't be able to hear you." I looked back and glanced over the edge toward the bottom of the tower again, then turned back to Rayna. "You better give us more than an hour, it looks like a long trip down."

"Two hours," she said. "That is the most I will give you. And please, if anything goes wrong, please yell for me—maybe it will echo off the walls. Or, better yet, shoot a ball of Ice up here or something. I will be here, watching."

"Thanks, Rayna. We should be okay. Remember, our only problem at the Pointing Finger was Raspy tricking us."

"Ummm, did you forget the earthquake and eruption of the volcano?" she said.

"Oh. Yeah. Okay, keep watch then."

I patted Joseph on the shoulder, and we began the long trip down the flight of steps—a staircase of salty water. I went first, with Joseph right behind me. After weeks and weeks of wearisome voyage at sea, we were finally in the Tower of Air. A thousand squishy steps below us, the Third Gift waited.

We hoped.

CHAPTER 26

The Tower of Air

It took a while to get used to the jiggling nature of the water steps, and my stomach never quite agreed with the whole experience. But as we made our way down the tower, turning every thirty steps or so at the switchbacks, the indescribable awe of what we saw through the walls of air captured our every thought.

The aquarium analogy had been far more apt than I'd first reckoned.

We saw thousands of creatures in a full spectrum of colors. There were jellyfish, sharks, sea horses, eels, floating plant vegetation that I never knew existed—it was almost too good to be true. Marine life had always fascinated me, and there I was, witnessing it in a way that had never been done before.

At one point, what looked like a submarine approached, and a quick shot of fear filled me, but it was soon replaced by sheer wonder. It was a whale. We had traveled pretty deep by then, but we still caught a quick flash of the massive sea mammal, and I would never forget it.

But as awesome as it all was, it couldn't last forever. Soon, there was not enough light to see much at all, and we had to settle for dark blue walls of water that approached blackness. Joseph slid his backpack off his shoulder and grabbed the flashlights, handing one to me. We flipped them on.

I tried shining it out into the water, but it didn't penetrate the murkiness very well. We continued our journey, step by step, mostly in silence.

Neither of us bothered to count the steps or switchbacks, but it was a long and tiresome task. I was already dreading the trip back up, wondering if we would even have the legs for it. Once or twice I was tempted to just grab Joseph and jump over the edge, relying on the Shield to protect us when we hit bottom. But somehow, that just didn't seem right, so I ignored the thought and kept going, one wiggly step after another.

Every now and then a spurt of water would shoot out of the wall beside us, like a sprung leak in a submarine. More often than not it would be below or above us, but one time it hit Joseph right in the head.

"Yeoooow! That's cold!" he said.

"Why is it doing that?" I asked.

"I'm not sure, but it doesn't seem good. The Givers told me that the Tower was failing, but I didn't know what they meant." He placed his hand in the spray of water still coming from the "leak" that had gotten him wet. "I hope it doesn't mean this whole thing is going to come collapsing down on top of us."

He looked at his watch.

"How long have we been at it?" I asked.

"About an hour, now." He paused and looked up. "If Rayna meant what she said about two hours, she'll be coming after us far before we're through. But hopefully by then we'll at least be on our way back up there."

I paused to take a look up to where we had come from. A small square of bright blue marked the top of the tower, and it surprised me how far we'd come. I could make out several streams of ocean water that were bursting through the walls of air, again reminding me of the submarine analogy. My stomach turned a bit, as a reverse fear of heights swamped my innards. I quickly looked back down and tried to will it away.

"You know," I said to Joseph, "I just thought about this, but do you think the walls of air keep going up forever after they break out of the water?"

"What do you mean?"

"Well, I just mean I wonder how tall the Tower of Air is— how far up it actually goes. Maybe it reaches all the way to the sky, and clouds part and go around it. Maybe planes feel a slight bump when they fly through it. I don't know, just a thought."

"Yeah," was all Joseph could say, breathing quite heavily. He was even more exhausted than I was.

We resumed our silence for another few minutes, and then almost stumbled when we suddenly ran out of steps and found ourselves on a bed of sand and rock.

We were at the bottom.

⁕

The water stairs ended in a corner of the square tower, so we had just been expecting another switchback. But it was a relief to have arrived somewhere, and know we didn't have to go any further. The bottom of the Tower of Air was indeed the bottom of the ocean itself, a soft floor of dry sand, littered with wet spots caused by falling spray from the leaks above. There was no vegetation of any kind, and no living things at all that we could tell. It was just a very large, square area of earth, with the towering walls of water looming above it like four ancient oracles.

"This is it?" I asked to no one in particular.

"What did you expect, a welcoming committee?" Joseph said. "The Givers would not have built such a thing for no reason, so let's not give up so easily. Come on, let's have a look-see."

We decided to walk along each wall and then cross the floor of the tower in crisscross patterns until we found something. Both of us had flashlights in hand, switched on. As we started down the first wall of water, I ran my free hand along the wet surface, feeling the cold water collect on my fingers and palm, like rubbing morning dew off of a car's hood. About halfway down the length of the wall, a thin line of spray shot out right in front of me—another leak. I walked around it and continued examining the wall of air for any sign of something different. The whole place was cold and creepy.

We came to the next corner with no incident except for a couple of more leaks, which appeared to be occurring more often. A heavy weight of panic began to surge up, but I repressed it. If the whole thing came crashing down, I would have the Shield to protect me. Joseph might take an unwanted bath if he were very far from me, however, and would never survive without my Shield to protect him.

The second wall showed nothing of interest, just wet darkness.

We saw the hole in the third wall before we even started walking along it.

It had been easy to miss in the darkness.

It was a second tunnel of air, this time horizontal, entering the depths of the dark world of water.

❧

The entrance to the tunnel was perfectly round, like the doors in a village of Hobbits. I shone my flashlight down its length, and could see no end to it. The curved walls were exactly the same as the flat planes of the square Tower, repelled into its shape by the magic air. The tunnel was tall enough to walk through at full height.

"You were right, Joseph, we found something."

"Good golly, I don't know if I can go in there," he said.

"Why?"

"Well, it's all fine and dandy in the Tower—at least I know there's a patch of the world up there somewhere. Once we go in there, I think I'm gonna go nuts with claustrophobia."

"Joseph, you were the one who insisted on coming down— Rayna would have loved to take your place." I smacked him on the back. "Now get a hold of yourself, old boy. If a little squirt like me can do it, surely you can."

"Easy for you to say, Mister nothing-can-hurt-me-because-of-my-big-bad-Shield."

But we both knew he would go in with me. It was almost a relief to see him scared a bit; it made my uneasiness a little more bearable. This was not some dumb movie, after all, and we were not fearless superheros. We were just normal people thrown into something that would scare the pants off the bravest man.

With our flashlights beaming like two swords of light, we entered the tunnel.

There was no sound except for the occasional hiss of a sprung leak as we walked down the sandy path. The leaks were much harsher on our nerves while traveling the tunnel, knowing that trillions of gallons of water hung right above our heads. I could tell that Joseph was a mess, his bald head glistening with sweat.

"Joseph," I said, "you need a towel or something? You've got more water on your pasty head than I've got hair on mine."

"Jimmy, when did you turn into such a smart alec? Once this is all over, I'm gonna teach you a lesson or two."

"Probably has something to do with being around Tanaka all the time," I said. "That guy is a hoot."

"Speaking of that strange bird, remember when he got all freaky that one night after mentioning those monkey things?"

"Yeah, I hadn't thought about that in a while." He really had been weird that night, and no one had said a word about it since. "I wonder if it has something to do with . . ."

"What?" Joseph asked when I trailed off.

"I'll tell you later. Look."

We had come to the end of the tunnel, and the air opened up into a huge cavern, probably fifty feet tall and a hundred feet in diameter, although it was impossible to tell because our flashlights were not quite strong enough to reach the opposite side. It reminded me of the cavern under the Pointing Finger, although its shape was the only similarity. There were no lava pools, and there was no stone. But there was something in the very middle of the watery cave.

It looked like a wooden door.

CHAPTER 27

The Two-Way Door

It was a door, but its placement made no sense.

The same size and shape as the other doors that had led to my first two Gifts, this one was standing upright in the middle of the sandy floor, but it had to be a trick of the eye. There was nothing supporting the door-no structure built around it, no beams holding it up, no wires attached. And it didn't appear to be buried in the ground either. The door just stood there, perfectly straight and upright, looking like it should fall down. There were iron handles on both sides.

Joseph and I walked up to it. I touched its wooden surface, its handles, and it all felt very solid. I walked around it, looking at it from all directions. It was just a door, standing there, leading to nowhere. What was its purpose? What good would it do me to walk through it? I would only step through and be in the same place—it didn't make sense.

I caught myself. Did a door in the middle of the woods make any sense, or one inside a volcano? When I received the Gift of Ice, Farmer had said something about how we weren't really in the volcano—that the door was some kind of a gateway to a magic place where I could meet him.

So despite what my eyes were telling me, I probably just needed to walk through it and I would end up somewhere else.

"What do you think?" I asked Joseph.

"I . . . guess you should go through the door. What else is there to do? And I know that this is where my part ends, from what I've heard about your other experiences." He smiled his normal Joseph grin. "Good luck, little buddy."

I shook his hand, for what reason I have no idea. Then I turned, put my hand on the iron handle, and took a deep breath. I was just about to pull it open when a strange voice echoed off the watery walls—a metallic, slithering sound.

"I would not do that if I were you."

I pulled my hand off the handle and looked around for the source of the voice. At first I thought it might be Joseph, but the look on his face proved me wrong. He was as baffled as I was, searching the cavern for any sign of our mystery speaker. Plus, the voice would have been impossible for Joseph to imitate—it was just not . . . human. It was the way I would imagine a snake would sound if it could talk, put through some kind of electronic manipulation.

It scared me to death.

Joseph and I walked around the door and the cavern, searching every inch of the place, but we didn't see anyone. I was just about to explain it away as a trick recording or something left by the Givers when a swift wind began to blow, twisting particles of sand into a mini-tornado over by one of the walls of the cavern. The tornado moved closer to the wall, and then they touched. The spinning wind pulled water out of the ocean, through the wall of air and into the tornado, until a tall funnel of blue water formed, spiraling with increasing rapidity. It moved away from the wall once it was roughly the size of a man.

Then, as we watched in astonishment, the twirling water ceased to spin, and became an elongated bubbly mass. Seconds later it took on definition, forming the image of a grown man, shimmering reflections traveling up and down its length. Before long, there was a person made completely of water standing in front of us, staring with translucent, wet eyes.

"Thank you for heeding my advice," it said with the voice of wet electricity. "Sorry I'm a bit late—I'd given in to the notion that no one would ever come to this place."

When it spoke, its lips moved like molten silver, its body glowing like liquid crystal. I was battling inside my head trying to convince myself that what stood before me was not some freak apparition of my imagination.

"You're . . . late?" I asked.

"Well, yes, obviously I am late. I am just appearing while you have been here long enough to do a fool thing like opening that door before I've spoken with you."

"Are you . . . real?" I asked.

"Dear boy, have a gander, will you? Do I look real to you? For pity's sake, can you not see that I am made out of water? Of course I am not real!" The watery man shook his head, and threw up his arms in impatient disgust.

"If you're not real," Joseph said, "then how are you standing here, speaking to us?"

"Do you not know the name of this place?" he asked.

"Well . . . yeah. The Tower of Air."

"And do you think the Givers go around naming things for no particular reason than to sound nifty?"

"Well—"

"Air! That is what forms me, that is what creates my voice. It is a powerful thing, air. Very powerful indeed."

"What is your purpose here?" I asked. "Why did you stop me from going through the door—how do we even know you're really a messenger from the Givers?"

"What, do I look like a Shadow Ka to you, boy? I may be a temporary configuration of water particles fashioned by anomalous wind inertia, but have some manners! I'm here to help you."

For some reason, his last statement relieved any lingering sense of fear, and I realized that I was beginning to like this guy.

"Next thing you'll be saying is that I'm 'all wet,' a tiresome pun that I hope to never hear again. Now, come, we all know the Tower is failing, and that our time is short." He walked over to us, his legs making gurgled sounds with each step. "I have been placed here, in this place, to give you one message. It is about this door."

He lifted his right arm, indicating the erect door in the middle of the cavern.

"You don't need me to tell you that it is rather unusual for a door to be standing in this manner in the middle of a room, much less at the bottom of the ocean in a cavern of air. You can enter this door from either direction—from the north, over there," he pointed, "or from the south, over there," he pointed to the opposite side.

"The direction you choose will determine the place to which you will go. One will kill you, the other will bring you to the Third Gift—which is quite fascinating if I may interject on that point."

He fell silent.

"Well," I finally said, "are you going to tell us how we can figure out which way is the right one?"

"What? Oh! Yes, yes, of course. Sorry, I was having an old daydream of mine, the one where I get swallowed by a mermaid. Now, where were we? Ah yes, the door." He paused, and put a glistening finger to his lips.

"As you well know by now, the Givers are mysterious, and love to speak in riddles. It's more annoying than having sand in your underpants, but I promise you, there is a definite purpose to it. Riddles can teach us, can make us smarter—they help us better understand and appreciate things once we figure them out. Wouldn't you agree?"

I nodded, but felt a feeling of dread as I remembered the last riddle I'd had to live through. The thought of those flying spears and the crumbling rift made me shudder.

"I am only a messenger," the apparition continued, "and nothing more, so let's get on with it, shall we? Are you ready?"

"Ready for what?" I asked.

"Why, the *Riddle of the Infinite Door.*"

CHAPTER 28

Riddle of the Infinite Door

"Come with me to the wall of water."

We followed the apparition's fluid gait over to the edge of the cavern, and he raised his hands, palms out, facing the water. Then he began to speak his riddle. As he spoke with metallic clicks and hissed vowels, raised letters formed on the wall—watery words that were easy to read in the glare of the flashlights.

And this is what we heard and read:

If I am lying, I tell you no lie
If I am truthful, believe me and die
What I say first, is good but not true
What I say second, is what you should do
Go from the north, but not from that way
Go forward not backward, and you'll save the day

Joseph and I stared, in awe of our own stupidity. It made no sense whatsoever.

"Well," the messenger said, "I must be off now that my duty is complete. All those hundreds of years, waiting for this. A bit anticlimactic, I must say. Adieu." Its shape began to distort back into blobs of water.

"Wait!" I yelled. In an instant it again formed into the tall man.

"That's it?" I asked. "What if we need help—will we ever see you again? Do you even have a name?"

"Why . . . yes, I have a name. Although it is rather embarrassing, I must say."

"What is it?" asked Joseph.

"Well, it's . . ." he hesitated. "Well, if you must know, I am called Scott."

I laughed—it was too good to be true.

"Scott?" I said through my chuckle. "Scott? You're a magic being made out of water and the best you could come up with was Scott?"

"Yes. I think it sounds rather distinguished—much better than *Jimmy*. Your parents really had to stay up all night thinking of that one. Now, I've had quite enough. Good-bye."

A gust of wind came from nowhere, and Scott exploded into a million pellets of water, blowing into the wall of the cavern like a quick burst of machine-gunfire. Just like that, our watery friend was gone. Surprising myself, I felt sad to see him go.

Joseph and I looked at each other and laughed, then looked over at the riddle. That sobered us right up.

Now all we had to do was figure it out.

The Riddle of the Infinite Door.

I figured we at least had a fifty-fifty chance of survival.

Joseph had been thinking the same thing.

"Well," he said, "there are only two ways to go through that door, so even if we just guessed, we'd have a fifty percent chance of being right." He walked over to it, and ran his palm along its wooden face on the south side.

"Yeah," I said, "but if you knew for a certainty that you also had a fifty percent chance of being killed, would you do it?"

"Sure, no problem." He smiled. "But of course, it's not me that's going through, now is it?"

"No, it's not. So if you don't mind, I'd like to be the one who decides to so carelessly throw my life away. Come on, between the two of us, this thing will be a piece of cake."

We went over to the wall with the raised lettering of water, and stood directly in front of the riddle.

"All right," Joseph said. "I've got an idea. Let's just look at it, both in silence, for ten minutes. That way we can think without being interrupted or influenced by each other. When the time is up, we'll discuss whatever ideas popped in our heads."

"Sounds good."

Joseph looked at his watch, and we began the thinking process.

When the ten minutes were up, we were closer to solving the Jack the Ripper case than we were to figuring out the meaning of the cryptic words.

"Now, now, we can do this," Joseph said. "Let's take it one line at a time." He pointed to me. "You read it out loud, then let's talk about it."

"All right. *If I am lying, I tell you no lie.*"

"Okay," Joseph said, "so it's like opposite day on that old kids show you used to make me sit through. If we think the riddle is lying, then it's actually the truth. Make sense?"

"If I ever watched that, I sure don't remember. How old was I?"

"I don't know, three or four. I still don't understand how you could've forgotten a guy like me. Go on, read the next line."

"*If I am truthful, believe me and die.*"

"See! What I said makes sense. Opposite day. We basically need to believe the riddle if it lies, and ignore it if it tells the truth."

"If you say so," I said. Joseph gave me an ugly look, and I let him know I was kidding. "No, that makes sense. Kind of. Okay, here's the next one. *What I say first, is good but not true.*"

"Wait." Joseph rubbed his chin, which had way more hair on it than his head did. "Go ahead and read the next line."

"*What I say second, is what you should do.*"

"Hmmmm. It's just about to click in the old ticker upstairs. Give me a second."

"Well," I said without waiting, "think about it. There are two more lines left, so those are the first and second things."

"Yeah, and it's telling us that the first one is good but not true!"

He looked at me, full of excitement, and I just stared back, not quite understanding.

"*Not true*, Jimmy! So the first thing is a lie, but good, and it told us that if it lies, it's actually not lying."

"Yeah, I think I'm getting it. And the second thing-it says that's what we should do. Meaning, it's the truth, so actually we should do the opposite, right?"

"I think so. Read the last two lines, which we've both agreed are what the riddle is referring to as the first and second things it says. Right?"

My mind was turning into oatmeal. "Uh, yeah. Here goes: *Go from the north, but not from that way.*" I paused, waiting for Joseph to say something. When he just stared, deep in thought, I continued, "*Go forward, not backward, and you'll save the day.*"

We said nothing for quite some time. I realized that my brain was not working as hard as it had when I was under the gun trying to solve the riddle for the Gift of Ice. I was relying on Joseph too much, using him as a crutch. My mind kind of shut down, and I found myself waiting for him to give me the solution.

More minutes passed.

"HA!" Joseph's voice exploded from his mouth, just about making me jump out of my undies.

"What?" I asked.

"Jimmy, my boy, how do you stand there, in my presence, and not bow down and praise me as the most brilliant man who has ever lived? I am utterly wise beyond even my own expectations. I've figured it out!"

"Yeah, you're the smartest person alive. Now tell me what you've come up with."

"You must do the first thing, because it is a lie and therefore not a lie." He began to pace the cavern, one arm behind his back, one hand raised with pointed finger as he made his various points. He looked like a ridiculous version of a college history professor.

"Therefore," he continued, "you enter from the north. But not *from* that way, you see. The second thing is what you should do and therefore not what you should do. You must go through the door *backward*. That explains how you can enter from the north, but not *from* the north, because you do not have your back to it. Your back will be to the south while you walk backward through the door, from the north but not really, and then receive your magnificent gift."

He took in a very deep breath and waited for my response, as proud as if he'd just revealed the cure for cancer. I gave up.

"Joseph, my brain hurts. The Givers sent you as my guide for this, and the things you just said seem to make sense—although I'm not sure I could repeat them for a million dollars. I think I'll just trust you on this one."

"No, my boy," he said, growing very serious. "This is far too important for you to take my word for it. I want you to explain it back to me, or I won't let you get near that door."

Frustrated, but knowing him to be right, I concentrated my powers of the mind, and combined the words in front of me with the things I'd just heard from Joseph.

"All right. There are six lines to the riddle, right?" Joseph nodded, even though what I had said was obvious.

"Okay, okay," I said with the voice of a man trying to build the nerve to bungee jump off a cliff. I rubbed my hands together. Then I walked up to the wall and pointed at each line of the riddle as I referred to it.

"The first and second lines say to follow a lie and do the opposite of truth. The third line says that the fifth line is a lie, so we must do it, according to the first line. The fourth line says that the sixth line is the truth, so we should do the opposite, according to the second line.

"So if I follow the counsel of the fifth line, combined with doing the opposite of the sixth line, then I will enter the door from the north, but backward, so that I am facing north, but also departing it."

I took my own deep breath, and looked over at Joseph.

"Well," he said, "if we had some chocolate cake, we could celebrate with cake and ice cream, if we had some ice cream."

"What?"

"Nothing. Come on."

He grabbed my shoulder and led me over to the door, walking around it in a complete circle, then coming to a rest on the north side. For a few moments we both just stared at the door. It resembled the other doors I'd been through to perfection—a rectangle but with slightly curvy edges, ancient wood, and strange etchings that were no longer recognizable. The iron handle was long and curved, vertical, and attached at both ends to the wood. It was a door that was ready to be opened.

"All right, Jimmy. This is it. I will be right here, waiting patiently. Say hello to the old man if he's the one in there, okay? I sure like that fellow—he reminds me of my granddad. Anyway, off with you now."

I took one more breath of the moist, salty air, and grabbed the iron handle. I looked over my shoulder at Joseph.

"Both times before, something terrible happened right after I finished. Be on your toes."

I pulled the door open, turned to face Joseph, and stepped through, backward.

CHAPTER 29

Farming in the Desert

A wave of sweltering heat hit me from behind. My back foot stepped on something soft and grainy, then my other foot followed. I could sense a brightness coming from behind me, and saw a look of wonder on Joseph's face, his eyes the size of silver dollars. Without a word, I pulled the door closed, and saw his face swept away by the aged wood.

The door did not disappear—for some reason I had thought it might. But I could tell right away that in this new place, the door stood in the open just like it had in the watery cavern. When I turned around to catch my first glimpse of the Third Gift's sanctuary, I sucked in dry, scorching air as I saw that this place couldn't be any more different from the one I'd left on the other side of the door.

I was not in a room. I was not in a building. I was outside, in the middle of a vast and never-ending desert.

A sea of orange, glowing sand flowed in undulating dunes everywhere I looked, extending to the distant horizon in all directions, meeting the blue sky with a crisp and defined line. The air was stifling, a slight breeze blowing it into my face like dragon's breath. It was a place that was everything I would have imagined the Sahara being like.

There was an absolute silence in the desert world for the few minutes I took in my surroundings. But then I heard a strange buzzing sound, a rumbling hum that was growing louder. I set off in that direction to investigate, my feet slipping and sliding in the loose sand.

The land rose sharply into a tall dune about twenty feet to the side of the door, and the sound was coming from there, getting louder by the second. I scrambled up its loose slope, putting my hands in front of me, grasping the hot sand, mostly in vain. The sand stuck to my wet shoes. I was three feet from the top when something big and monstrous flew off of the dune from the other side, flying over my head and crashing to the ground behind me. I spun to get a look.

It was a dune buggy.

The four-wheel, glorified go-cart was revving its engines. It had landed and turned around so that it was now facing me. The driver of the desert machine was wrapped fully in white linens, his head wrapped as well, protecting him from sand and sun. I had a very good idea of who this person was, but I sure hadn't expected him to greet me this way.

He cut the engine, and swung his legs out of the vehicle. He walked over to me, paused, then lifted his hand to pull away the cloth covering everything but his eyes. As his arm went to his face and he pulled back the linen, I could see a very familiar plaid pattern.

He revealed his face, then pulled what seemed like a whole

houseful of bed sheets off his body. Dusty overalls and plaid flannel met my eyes. No surprise this time—it was Farmer— the mysterious Giver who had become my mentor and friend.

"Hello, Jimmy," he said.

"Hello to you. Is it your goal to make sure each of our meetings is always stranger than the one before it?"

"Oh, come now, child of the Four Gifts. I may be a figment of your imagination, and I may be an old man, but no one said I couldn't have a little fun." He smiled and indicated the buggy behind him. But his words had made my heart pause.

"Figment of my imagination? What do you mean?"

Farmer's face grew serious, then broke back into a smile. "Oh, it's nothing like what it sounds, believe me. I am most definitely real, as real as your hand, as real as your heart, as real as your house back in Georgia. But when we meet in these special places, I am more of a recording than anything else. It's very difficult to understand, much less explain."

He turned and walked back toward his vehicle, indicating with a wave of the hand that he wanted me to follow. I did, again finding it difficult to walk in the shifty sand.

Farmer reached into the buggy and pulled out an old lawn chair, then gave it to me.

"Go ahead," he said, "have a seat. We have a lot to discuss, and you are getting closer and closer to knowing the full truth of things. Very close indeed."

I grabbed the chair and unfolded it, reminded of summer barbecues and little league baseball games. It took a little working, but I eventually got the chair settled and stable in the soft sand, then sat down. I was very eager to learn more.

Just as he had in the room of ice inside the Pointing

Finger, Farmer sat down on an invisible chair. He leaned back, and put one foot up on his knee, looking like a man ready to watch the big football game.

"My dear boy, I cannot convey to you how happy it makes me to see you arrive here. You have come so far, through so much of danger and worry." He let his foot drop to the ground and leaned forward. "I am very anxious to tell you more. I think you are prepared more than ever now."

He leaned back, his look of excitement fading.

"However, it also drains me to tell you some of the things I must. No matter what you have been through, you cannot be prepared for the surprises that are in store for you. You have seen much that has forever changed your perceptions of the world and the universe itself. But it truly has only been the beginning."

"Farmer," I said, "you always tell me that you are going to tell me everything, but it sure seems like you never do. What is a Stomper? When are they coming and what will they do to us? I feel like I need to know these things—everything. How else am I supposed to defeat them?"

A gentle wind picked up, blowing grains of sand lightly across the back of my neck. It was very strange that I had not even paused to think how weird it was that I had stepped into a desert through a door standing on the bottom of the ocean.

"I have told you before," Farmer said, "how there is rhyme and reason to my timing on revealing the secrets of the Stompers to you. You have been patient, and I thank you. But listen to me." He pointed his finger at me like an executioner. "If I had told you everything in the beginning, you would not be here. You would never, ever have made it this far. And that has a much different meaning than you probably think."

"See!" I said. "Again with the riddles! What are you talking about?"

"I understand your impatience. Perhaps you are ready. I will tell you everything if time permits, but I want first to bestow something on you, to ensure that it happens before the tides of trouble rise on this sea of sand. You know how our luck has been thus far . . ."

"You mean the Third Gift?"

"Of course I do."

He stood and walked to the back of the dune buggy and opened a small compartment. He pulled a small object out and came back to sit on the chair that was not there. I tried to see what he held, but it was cupped in both hands, hidden from view.

I couldn't believe the feeling that consumed me, a tingling excitement that swelled inside of me. The Third Gift. The Third Gift! I thought about how much the other two had completely changed my life, and here I was about to receive the next one. I could hardly stand it.

"Now," Farmer said. "I told you once before that the second two Gifts were much different from the first two. This is very, very true. But I assure you that each of the Four have their own very distinct purpose in the end. Indeed, I bet you couldn't guess the Fourth Gift—the most powerful one—if I gave you one billion chances." He let out a little chuckle, like this was all some game to him.

"Come on, Farmer, please." I had no time to worry about the final Gift right then.

"All right, boy. I say, you have grown up considerably since that day under the door in the woods. Grown up, indeed."

He pushed his cupped hands out from his lap until they

were directly in front of me. Then he revealed what was lying within. A piece of iron, shaped like a crescent moon with an open crevice going down the middle. It looked like an open pea pod made out of cold metal, or a canoe built by an ancient civilization. Four oval objects were placed along the curved opening running down its length.

They were four red beans.

"You must eat each one," Farmer said, "all together. I think you will find them quite tasty."

"What are they? What do they taste like?"

"I believe they are similar to . . . cooked peas, if I'm not mistaken."

My face turned the color of those demonic spheres of foul flavor called peas that my mom insisted on cooking at least once a week.

"Peas?"

Farmer laughed. He seemed very cheerful for the circumstances.

"I'm only teasing you, Jimmy. Your friend, the one called Joseph, told me you had a certain dislike for that cuisine. Do not worry, it has no taste, just like the other Gifts you have partaken. As for what the Gift can do, eat and I will tell. Surely you trust me by now?"

I only nodded, and then reached down and picked up the four beans. They were heavier than they appeared, their sports-car-red surface shiny and slippery. I almost dropped them. I allowed them to fall into the cup of my palm, then rattled them, looking up at Farmer with a sarcastic raising of my eyebrows.

"I don't know, do I trust you? If you spent too much time with Joseph, this is probably some practical joke food that tastes like dog-doo and then you'll give me the real Gift after I've puked all over the sand."

Farmer smiled and assured me that was not the case.

I popped the beans into my mouth and chewed the tasteless morsels. They were the texture and consistency of jellybeans, without the sweet flavor. I finished and swallowed with a big gulp, then looked at Farmer expectantly.

"Well?"

"Ah yes, the Third Gift. The only thing that will amaze you more than this Gift is the promise I make to you that the Fourth Gift is more powerful."

"Really? What is this one called?"

"It is called the . . ." He paused. I waited.

Farmer leaned in for effect, his shaggy-bearded face only inches from mine.

"The Anything."

CHAPTER 30

The Third Gift

"Wow, that does sound impressive," I said. "The Anything? What . . . what could that possibly mean?"

Farmer stood up.

"You know the drill. Come, follow me."

We walked, or stumbled up the dune that he had flown over to greet me when I'd first arrived. When we crested the sandy wall, I was shocked to see a massive pile of enormous granite boulders, stacked as high as a two-story building, and wider than a city bus. We walked up to its very edge, and I scanned the mammoth heap of stone.

"What is this?"

"Jimmy, raise your right arm."

I looked at him in disbelief. "Are you serious? I think I've learned that point already—that the Gifts are as easy as raising your arm."

He was not smiling.

"I am very serious. If you cannot be trusted to obey such a simple thing, how can we rely on you to do what it takes to save an entire world? Sometimes we are asked to do things for reasons we do not fully understand."

Humbled, I did as he asked.

"Now, the other arm. Please, raise it."

I did.

"Now, listen with great care. This Gift will take much discipline and foresight. You cannot take it lightly. You see, the name of this Gift explains it quite well. My boy, you can literally do anything."

I said nothing, trying to understand.

"There are only two conditions," he continued. "First, it cannot be used to maim, alter, or kill other living beings, even against the most malicious of enemies. You will regret that some day, I assure you."

"What . . . what do you mean, I can do anything?"

"I mean what I say; I say what I mean. Just as you have lifted your arms to the sky with nothing but thought, you can now do *anything*. If your mind can think it, the Gift can fulfill it. It is the Anything."

"But . . . how can that be? It seems too good to be true, too unbelievable. I'm having a hard time comprehending what you're talking about when you say I can do anything."

Farmer pointed to the stack of boulders, towering over us.

"I will help you learn how it works, of course. But then I must initiate the second condition, which is where the discipline I spoke of comes into play. Look at these rocks."

I did as he asked, and looked them up and down.

"I want you to pile these boulders, one on top of another in a single vertical line."

Then I said the only word one can say in such a situation: "What?"

"Come, now. You heard me. Stack them over there." He pointed to a flat spot to the right of where we stood. "With the Second Gift, you did not succeed the first time I tested you. I want you to pause and think, now, and succeed on your initial try. I will be over here." He walked back to the top of the dune and sat down in his pretend chair.

I took a couple of steps back, and felt myself sweating. It still made no sense to me, none whatsoever. Anything? What did that mean?

No, I told myself. Get a hold of things, Jimmy. You're not the kid who opened the door in the woods. Quit being one. Farmer was showing his faith in you, his belief in you. Prove yourself.

I looked at the rocks. I thought about the way my mind linked with the other Gifts, how my thoughts had guided the rebounding action of the Shield. The way they guided the direction and action of the Ice. It was no different with this new Gift—it couldn't be.

With a renewed sense of confidence, I called upon the Anything.

I pictured what Farmer had asked of me—a line of rocks, one on top of the other, starting with one and then shooting toward the sky in an impossible, balanced tower of stone. And then it started.

A great wind came from all directions, and the boulders began to dance.

CHAPTER 31

Stones of Discipline

The wind had the power of ancient gods it seemed, and moved the boulders like grains of sand caught in a whirlpool.

Rocks were shooting into the sky, everywhere, moving and revolving and taking position. A particularly large one lifted into the air, and floated over to the spot where I had imagined the tower and settled to the ground. Another rock came over and landed on top of the first one. By now all the boulders were floating in the air above us, joining together in a bizarre waltz of gravity-defying lumps of stone. One by one, they moved to the ever-lengthening tower of rocks, each settling on top of the one that preceded it.

It grew like Jack's beanstalk, higher and higher, no thicker than one boulder in any place. By the time the last rock had disappeared high above, it was the tallest structure I had ever seen.

"Okay, now," Farmer shouted, "Obliterate them all into fine sand, and blow them into the passing winds, never to be seen again."

I looked up, straining my neck in an attempt to see the top, but it was impossible.

"All right," I said.

With a flicker of thought, with a conjured image in my head, I did exactly what he instructed. The rocks exploded with a loud puff into a mist of fine sand, and were whisked away by the wind, a thick cloud of red quickly passing into oblivion.

I turned and faced Farmer, a huge smile on my face.

"Don't get too excited," he said, standing and walking over to where I stood. "Do not forget I have not told you everything."

"You mean the second condition?"

He nodded.

"What is it?"

He paused, making sure I understood that he was about to say something very important. Then:

"From this second on, you can only use the Anything four times."

"Four times," Farmer continued, "and it is gone forever. You will have to choose wisely."

Still overwhelmed by the sheer amount of newness regarding this Gift, I sat down on the sand, ignoring how dirty it was. Farmer had been right when he said that it would be different from the Ice and Shield. I could never have imagined it, or even dared to dream it. And the Fourth Gift was more powerful?

But I could only use the Anything four times. That made me nervous. How would I know when to call upon it, when it was important enough? Farmer sensed my questions.

"You have many trials still ahead—far more than four, I am afraid. You have grown and learned so much, Jimmy—I have much confidence that you will choose the times wisely that you call upon the Anything. But remember this, my friend: you must save one for the very end of this conflict. No matter what happens, no matter what terrible thing may occur, you must not use the last chance of the Anything."

He paused for a moment, his shaggy face hairs waving in the hot breeze.

"Therefore, choose how to use the first three with great caution."

The magnitude of the Gift was so fascinating, creeping to the forefront of my thoughts, that the worry of when to use it seemed secondary.

"Are there any limits to what I can use it for?"

"Well, I have already told you that it cannot be called upon to hurt or kill or even alter living beings. Not even the Shadow Ka. Other than that, its possibilities are end-less. You could move a mountain, empty the oceans, turn your shoes into cheese. I don't recommend the latter—not much value."

He smiled, as if he were my grandpa telling me the best way to hook a worm.

"I have one more question," I said. I pointed to where the rocks had been. "What about the thing I just did, stacking then destroying the rocks? Would that have been one usage or two?"

"Oh, it's not as complicated as it may seem. It is however your brain interprets it, I believe. In the case of the rocks, I would guess that would have counted as one time."

"You would guess?"

"It's *your* mind that controls it, child of the Gifts. You will know."

He slapped me on the thigh.

"Now, since nothing catastrophic has happened yet, perhaps we have time to discuss a few things."

He looked at me, his gaze needling into my eyes.

"It is time to tell you about the Stompers."

His face grew long and a haunted look shadowed his eyes.

"I am afraid they are entering your world even as we speak."

CHAPTER 32

The Stompers Revealed

Farmer stood and paced in circles around me as he spoke for the next few minutes, hands clasped behind his dirty overalls.

"When you blocked the Black Curtain, you merely delayed the inevitable, I am sorry to say. The world was already filled with thousands of Shadow Ka, far more than we had imagined, scattered throughout the earth like the pestilence they are. They had almost been ready to bring in the Stompers, but you prevented it from happening. At least for a time.

"That Blocking has weakened considerably. I have sensed several Rippings in the Curtain in the last few days, and the Stompers are pouring through them at a frightening rate. It is only a matter of weeks, perhaps months, before they rip the Curtain at will and come forth with all their might and malice. That will be a terrible day, and we must hasten our efforts to endow you with the Fourth Gift."

Farmer had not really said many words yet, but the amount of information contained within them was too much to compute. I didn't know what to ask first, but I had to say something.

"You mean . . . are you telling me that there are already Stompers on the earth?"

"Yes. Not many, not a fraction of what is coming, but yes, they have arrived."

"Okay, then, I think I am finally ready to know what they are."

"You think you are ready, but I have my doubts. I have worried about this day for a long time. For a very long time."

"Please, Farmer, tell me."

He put his hands into his denim pockets and let out a sigh.

"All right, Jimmy. I will tell you." Another pause. "The Stompers are your worst nightmares."

Frustration filled me. "I know, I know—that is all I hear about them! They are scary, they are horrible, they are worse than anything I can imagine. Just tell me what they are, please!"

Farmer looked disappointed in me, but then his expression transformed into a sad understanding.

"No, Jimmy, you are not hearing my words. I am not speaking in metaphors—there is no time for that now."

"What . . . what do you mean?"

"The Stompers *are* your worst nightmares."

CHAPTER 33

The Dream Warden

My complete silence said everything I was feeling.

"I know it is hard to comprehend. I have tried to warn you that our enemy is nothing like you expected. They have no visible substance to them, no tangible body to wage war against. Their evil Shadow Ka swoop in and prepare their next victims, frightening them, lulling them into a never-ending sleep that at first seems like an escape from the horrors that beset them. But then they are taken in their dreams to a place where the Stompers hold them forever.

"There, they live the rest of their existence in a world of terror, a world of pain, a world where every one of their worst nightmares is manifested—except they can never wake up again. Their fear is food unto the Stompers. It is their sustenance, their well-being, their livelihood."

Farmer collapsed to the ground, putting his head into his hands.

"Oh, Jimmy, it is a horrible, horrible thing." He began to weep, something I had never seen him do before. No words came to me—I was in a state of complete and unbreakable shock, trying my best to understand something that seemed impossible.

"You are our only hope, Jimmy—you are the first one in countless worlds to reach a point where you have a chance to defeat them, to save an entire world from their ruthless terror and hatred, however small that chance may be. And then, if you are successful . . ."

He trailed off, looking into the distance.

"No, we can only take one step at a time." He stood back up and regained his composure.

"I am sorry for becoming so emotional. I have just seen too many worlds fall to their evil, to their malice. So many good, wonderful beings, fallen under the Stompers' spell. But you can save your people, Jimmy. That is why we must hurry."

He walked over to me and indicated that I should stand. I did so, and he motioned to the door.

"You must go now, and find the Dream Warden."

"I think Joseph said something about . . . him, or her, or whatever."

"Yes, Joseph knows a little about the Warden. The Dream Warden is the only one who can put into play the final piece of the puzzle, the Fourth Gift. I cannot do it."

"Who is it? Where do I need to go?"

Farmer walked to the door, and I followed him. We stopped directly in front of it.

"I can only tell you that you must go to a place where there is no north, The Northless Point. There, in exactly three weeks from this moment, you will see a Ripping of the Black Curtain, one that we have planned just for you. The Rip will only stay open for fifty-six minutes, precisely."

"I have to go back into the Blackness?" I asked, dread filling me.

"Yes, and it is vital that you find what is needed and make it back to the Rip within the fifty-six minutes, or you will be stuck there for quite some time. The lady in the white dress, the Lady of the Storm, is there, through the Blackness, waiting for you. Our Ripping will take you to a place near the gateway to her world."

Farmer rubbed his temples, as if to fend off a headache. "When you go into her world, there is something you must remember. A host of Shadow Ka will be waiting for you. Now, we both know they cannot hurt you, but they can do something even worse."

"What do you mean?" I asked.

"The gateway inside the world of the Lady of the Storm is very fragile, as you will see when you get there. The Ka know you must go to that world, and they will be waiting, so that they can destroy the gateway after you have arrived. If this happens, you will be stuck there, in that world of storms, forever."

"Forever?"

"Yes, forever. But don't worry, I think you will be okay, because of your Shield—just not in the way you expect."

"Huh?" I asked, sounding like the dumbest kid in a class on how to count to one.

"I've told you before that you have not yet realized the extent of the Shield's powers, and it will have to help you in a new way when you go to the world of the Lady of the Storm. I will get back to that if we have time, but let's move on.

"Once you reach the Lady, she will reveal unto you what needs to happen in order for you to find the Dream Warden, who will in turn reveal to you how to obtain the final Gift. If you do not make it to this place, all will be for naught.

"Everything depends on the Dream Warden. Everything."

As he said these last words, I noticed that it was getting darker, rapidly. I looked to the west, or the direction I thought was west, where the sun had been dipping to the horizon the last time I noticed.

A darkness was coming at us. I felt the blood drain from my face, and Farmer saw my skin turn pale. He followed my gaze.

A wall of black, writhing goo was fast approaching. It was ten stories tall and hundreds of feet wide, rolling along the ground toward us like a dust storm, picking up speed. It looked exactly like the substance that had chased me out of the place under the door in the woods back home.

"We should have known it was too good to be true," Farmer said. "Our enemies are never far away in these places. Quickly, now, through the door you go."

My questions dissipating like smoke in a stiff wind in light of the coming wall of death, I didn't argue. I pushed on the handle of the door.

It didn't budge. I pulled, even though I knew that to enter the desert world I had pulled the door into the wet cavern. Nothing. Looking behind me, I pushed and pulled again.

Death in the form of black goo was fast approaching.

And the door would not open.

CHAPTER 34

A Door in the Air

"Help me!" I yelled.

A great wind picked up, blowing from the other side of the door toward the oncoming wave of black behind us. I knew why. The goo sucked in life, devoured everything in its path, like a vacuum that was possessed. I'd learned that lesson back in Georgia.

Farmer pushed against the door with his shoulder, and I joined him. We put all of our strength into it, digging our heels into the sand that gave under our feet, slipping and sliding as we exerted every drop of energy we had.

The door opened an inch. Blue water poured through the bottom of the opening, about two feet high, soaking our legs and feet and turning the sand into mud. I had the horrible vision of the Tower of Air collapsing completely on the other side, drowning Joseph and probably Rayna, who had surely come looking for us by now.

I felt a rush of adrenaline, and I heaved my weight against the door. It moved another two inches, the water really gushing through as it did. The force of the water began to shut the door again. An arm shot through the opening, wedging itself through the space to keep it open.

Joseph's arm—he was still alive, at least for now. His face appeared.

"Hurry, Jimmy!" he said. "Push! The Tower is collapsing!"

The current of air had picked up considerably, the black wave getting closer by the second. The wind transformed then into something far more terrible—it was truly sucking at us now. My feet lifted from the ground without warning. I grabbed the edge of the door at the last second, holding on with wet, slippery fingers. I called upon the Ice and froze my hands to the wood, the rest of my body now parallel to the ground, the black goo's force pulling me with all its might.

Farmer had slipped and collapsed to the ground, his arms wrapped around the base of the door, choking and gasping under the pouring water. Neither of us were pushing against the door anymore.

"Joseph!" I yelled, "can you pull it open?"

"My arm . . ." was his reply. The door was hurting him badly.

Despair cascaded through my body. I stole a glance behind me, and saw that the black wave would be on us in less than a minute. It had grown so large I could barely see anything else but writhing, hungry darkness.

Then it got worse.

A grating, snapping sound came from below, masking Farmer's wet grunts of exertion. The door and its frame shifted, tilting to the right several inches. I looked down, my body flapping in the wind like a flag.

The door was ripping from its foundation, Farmer barely hanging on to its tattered bottom corner that had come loose. I froze his hands to the door as well, and was just about to yell again to Joseph when the whole structure tore free.

The door flipped and shot into the air, towing Farmer and I along with it, our hands firmly frozen in place.

We were airborne, a flat door with two figures trailing it like hung laundry, headed straight for the middle of the black wave.

I knew we only had seconds.

The door still acted in every way like an opening into the water cavern. Water poured from the thin opening, swept away in a horizontal stream. Joseph's arm was also there, keeping the door open.

"Jimmy," he said, struggling to be heard over the roar of the wind and water, "one more try, one more push! You can do it, boy!"

We were in a slow roll as we approached the wall of black. My stomach turned and pitched, my head swam. Farmer had somehow gotten a leg up against the door, and was pushing with it as hard as he could. I released my left hand from the Ice and did my best to push against the door as well, pulling against the frame with my right hand for leverage. I could see Joseph's other hand clasped along the edge, pulling.

I could feel the darkness behind me, reaching out, waiting, hungry, sensing victory.

A quick thought flashed through me—*use the Anything*. But I didn't want to, not this early, with so much still ahead of us. Then I remembered my first Gift and had an idea.

I reared my head back, and with every possible ounce of strength still contained within my body, I heaved my head against the door, trying with all my effort to smash my brains out.

The Shield sprung into action. It slammed the door all the way open to protect me, a wall of water rushing outward. Joseph caught himself just before falling out—he had planted his feet firmly on the top edge of the doorframe. He grabbed my shirt, and pulled me inside the cavern below the ocean, skimming across the top of the river of water.

The force of the rushing river shut the door for the last time.

Farmer was left on the other side.

CHAPTER 35

Scott's Head Pops Up

The freezing water was already up to my chest as I tried my best to right myself in the frothing pool. Joseph grabbed my hand.

"Let's get out of here!" he yelled.

He let go of my hand and we swam toward the tunnel that led back to the Tower. The passageway was filling up fast—there were only a few feet between its curved top and the rising waters. My entire body was exhausted, and I had to reach deep down to find the strength to keep moving.

"Joseph," I said, spitting out salty water, "stay close to me. If it does collapse, the Shield will protect us somehow."

"Okay," he replied. He tread water for a second until I caught up with him, and then we continued on, side by side.

Just before we reached the entrance to the tunnel, a head popped up out of the water in front of us, blocking our way. The shock of it made my heart skip a beat, and I cried out in surprise. Then it registered in my head who it was.

"I have one last message for you," the watery face of gleaming crystal said.

It was Scott.

"The Giver is okay," he said. "He wanted you to know that. He cannot be touched in those special places where he meets you, and only hung around for as long as he did to help you. I sure hope you are grateful, Mr. Fincher."

After recovering from the sight of a face springing up out of the water, we continued swimming. Scott floated alongside us. His head bobbed up and down to our right, speaking as we swam.

"The Giver wanted me to tell you one last time what you must do, because with a brain like yours, he knew you needed to be told more than once."

It seemed like such an odd time for Scott to continue his smart aleck ways.

"Remember—go to the Northless Point, where there is no north, and enter the Blackness. Go through the nearest iron rings, find the Lady of the Storm, and she will direct you to the Dream Warden. You will only have fifty-six minutes. Good-bye!"

His head slipped under the water.

The strangeness of it all was lost in our panic to get out, but his message did help solidify the importance of Farmer's instructions, so I was grateful. I even had the thought that I would miss the watery creature.

We continued down the tunnel, our backs almost scraping its top now. The water had become almost unbearably cold, and I knew the Shield would kick in soon to protect me. But I had learned from my first spill into the ocean—to save my dad—that it was very difficult to move through the water when the Shield encased me. My brain was holding it off for as long as possible.

We swam on. My limbs begged me to stop, and I could see that Joseph was just as tired. The cold bit our skin like small daggers. Water went up my nose and down my throat, burning and choking.

We swam on.

We entered the Tower of Air.

I tried to touch my feet to the ground for a brief rest, but the water was too high. Exhausted, I did my best to tread water, although my head dipped down below the surface more than once. I looked around to take in our surroundings.

On every wall of the tower, millions of leaks sprayed forth water in varying degrees of strength, raining down on us in a mighty deluge. And then I noticed something that brought a wave of sick despair to my innards.

The stairs were gone.

CHAPTER 36

Heavy Water

Joseph forgot the urgency of staying together and thrashed his way over to the wall where we knew the stairs had ended their journey from far above. He felt along the wet wall, fighting the incessant spraying that was coming from leaks everywhere.

He yelled something, but I didn't hear. My body was finally giving up—all I wanted was a minute to rest my bones. I sunk beneath the surface.

The Shield popped open a bubble of protective air around me. I floated all the way down until I was lying on the ocean floor, sinking slightly into the muddy quagmire the seething waters had formed. I rested my head on my arms, desperate for just a small rest.

A terrible sound yanked me from my respite.

I had never been to Niagara Falls before, but TV shows about them had always fascinated me. The roar of the falls was my favorite part, and I'd longed to go there since I was a little teeny squirt of a kid. It was that awesome noise, the sound and reverberation of the entire world collapsing in a severe torrent of cascading water, which I heard at that moment.

I looked up, and there was no blue sky in the distance, no mist, no rainfall from the leaks. The entire ocean was falling down on top of us like a falling tidal wave. Right before it hit us, I heard two people scream.

Two people.

One was Joseph. The other came from a familiar source— I had heard it for the first time while up in Ole Betsy, when I had seen her mistreated by the evil Mayor Duck.

Somehow, Rayna had joined us, and I had no idea how I could possibly get to her and Joseph before it all ended.

❧

The Shield protected me, but the fright of seeing millions of tons of water falling on top of you was impossible to ignore. I instinctively covered my face and held my breath while the roar and explosive splashing surrounded me. Despite the awesome power of the Shield, my protective bubble still swayed in the massive current created by the waterfall. My fear for Joseph and Rayna consumed me, and I stood up and moved as best as I could around the floor of the ocean, the pocket of air following.

I knew a little about ocean stuff, and I felt for sure that the other two could never survive the pressure that much water creates. I worried that they might be dead already. I cried out for them, knowing it was useless.

The swirling waters began to calm, all the empty spaces filled now, the ocean going on its normal way as a big tub of dirty water. A claustrophobic panic attacked me, not only for my friends, but for me. How was I going to swim to the surface?

The Ice, I could use the—

Then it hit me. I had a third Gift now, one that was almost all-powerful. Every time I used it had to be of the utmost importance, to fulfill the direst need. For a second I hesitated, realizing that the fate of the entire world rested on my shoulders, wondering if two people were worth using one of the four chances I would have.

My dad used to always say that the needs of the many outweighed the needs of the few, but sometimes, in special circumstances, it went the other way. I'd always thought it very profound until my mom told me he'd stolen it from a Star Trek movie.

A small nugget of peace erupted in my heart, and I knew that I could not change who I was, or the way I thought. Joseph and Rayna were my friends.

I closed my eyes and called upon the Anything.

CHAPTER 37

First Chance Gone

For a second or two I imagined the way I wanted it to happen, imagined the waters swirling apart and forming another void in the water. But then I stopped myself. Farmer had said my brain was in charge, that it would decide how it worked and what constituted one usage of the Gift. So I changed my strategy.

All I did was make it very clear, and imagined it, envisioned it in my head, that I wanted the three of us safely on the boat again, alive and well. Then, just as I did with the other Gifts, I *thought* it into action.

Some unseen force exploded beneath me. With the Shield acting as the prow of a ship, it parted the water before me as I shot toward the surface. The sensation of flying through water was breathtaking, and I allowed myself to enjoy it for the few seconds it lasted.

I broke the surface with a loud pop and swish, catapulting forty or fifty feet into the air. My stomach and lungs seemingly stayed in the ocean, because I couldn't breathe. I looked around and saw two other figures in the air with me, and for a split second we all hung there, looking at each other. The three of us were meteors in reverse, trailing streams of water still connecting us to the ocean.

Then a great wind came from nowhere, and lifted us into its arms, swirling around us, holding us, carrying us with a gentle but massive sigh of air to the waiting ship below. Soon, to the shock of our companions who happened to be on the decks, we were placed without harm onto the yacht, safe as can be.

My only regret was that I didn't have a camera to capture the look on Rusty's face.

Mom threw her arms around me and didn't let go for the longest time. During our reunion, I thought about what just happened.

One down, three uses of the Third Gift to go. It was a little discouraging, but if given the same chance a million times, I would've saved my friends without fail. But the power of the Anything was more than we realized.

Joseph and Rayna both told us that a pocket of air had formed around them as the water crashed down to the ocean floor. That meant, as far as we could tell, that the Anything could actually work *before* I invoked it, that it could somehow see into the future. Either that, or it could go back in time to fulfill its beckoning call. Either way, we were all relieved it had worked so well.

Rusty could not get over it. He kept going on and on about what it was like to see three bodies suddenly shoot out of the water then float down safely to the ship. If only we'd caught it on video.

The first thing I did after catching my breath was to check on Dad. He had not changed, still sleeping in his bed like a dead man. It made me ill now, knowing what I did about the Stompers. I still didn't understand how they worked, but the thought of Dad being infected by one of those things made me sick to the core. I spent some time with him and then went back to join the rest of the crew.

The remainder of the day was spent in the Mess Hall, resting and filling each other in on what had transpired since we'd set out on the raft. Joseph and Rayna and I went first, taking turns telling them everything. I told most of it, since I had been the only one to go through the door far below us.

Rayna had given us the two hours she had promised and then set out down the stairs, bent on saving us. She'd been wary of the many leaks, but it only increased her concerns over us, so she had kept coming. The stairs had collapsed when she was only twenty feet from the bottom, or else her fall would have surely killed her. When the Tower began to collapse, and we were all swimming around at the bottom, we'd somehow missed her in all of the commotion and noise. I couldn't help but wonder what would have happened if I had not heard her scream at the last second and therefore had not included her in my invoking of the Third Gift.

As for the ship itself, they had been able to sense the weakness in the Tower long before it imploded, so they'd taken the ship a little further out to avoid being sucked into the whirlpool its collapse caused. They knew they could do nothing but hope that my Gifts saved the day.

In the end, that was exactly what had happened.

Feeling safe once again, and warm, I told them that in the morning, I would give more details concerning what needed to happen next. They could see my exhaustion and did not argue. I also had not yet told them about the Stompers—I was just not ready for that.

I hit the sack. After what I had learned from Farmer, I was very glad that I did not dream that night.

CHAPTER 38

Tender Moment

The next morning we were huddled around our breakfast, all efforts at small talk quashed by the anticipation of what I would tell them next.

"All right, Jimmy-san," Tanaka said through his oily mustache, "please hurry with eggs and toast and tell what happened, for crying up loud, neh?"

We all laughed at his failed attempt at an American saying.

"What?" he roared.

"Okay, okay," I said, glad that he had kind of broken the ice. "Before Tanaka gets his eyebrows in a wad, I'll tell you."

I pushed my plate aside and folded my hands on the table in front of me. I leaned on my forearms, and tried to look at everyone as I spoke.

"The first thing we have to do is a little vague, because Farmer gave me another riddle." Everyone groaned.

"It's not so bad, guys. It doesn't sound as hard as the last one, really."

"What is it?" Miyoko asked.

173

"We have to go to a place where there is no north—in other words, a place called The Northless Point. Tanaka, if you can figure that one out, I'll give you a buck."

He snapped to attention, his finger whipping down from his face into his lap—we'd caught him in a suspicious itch of the nose.

"Yes," he said, "I start thinking right away."

"We have three weeks, I mean, two weeks and six days— twenty days. At that time a rip in the Black Curtain will appear, and I will have only fifty-six minutes in which to go in, find one of those iron gateways, and find some woman called The Lady of the Storm. She'll direct me on how to find this Dream Warden we've talked about, who will apparently reveal to me the Fourth Gift. Then I have to get back out before the Rip closes. All in fifty-six minutes."

There was a pause, the silence thick with contemplation.

The first thing all of us wanted to do was to get off the stupid ocean.

So it was decided. We would go back to Japan, where Geezer was supposed to have gathered as many of the Alliance as possible. Once there, we would somehow figure out where to find the Northless Point and—hopefully—obtain the Fourth Gift. Then, we could regroup and decide what needed to happen in order to win the battle against the Shadow Ka and the Stompers.

That point in time seemed so distant. When we spoke of it, none of us had any concept of what that battle would be like. We didn't even know if it was something that the

Alliance could help with, or if it was something I had to do on my own. But we could only take it one step at a time, and obtaining the Fourth Gift was the next item on the agenda. We hoped everything else would fall into place after that.

Of course, we should have known better.

The next morning, I sat at my favorite spot again, looking out into the great ocean from the front of the ship. We had nineteen days left now, and I couldn't believe how long that suddenly seemed. We had been at sea for weeks, even months, and now three weeks seemed like a lifetime.

Rusty joined me after a while. Since our little spat—if you could even call it that—we had not spoken much, and I could tell by his demeanor that he was about to set things straight. Even before he began, I was ashamed that I had not initiated this talk.

"Jimmy," he said, "you are looking at a complete fart-for-brains." I knew it was his bizarre way of apologizing, but I didn't let on.

"Oh, please, Rusty, what're you talking about?"

"I'm sorry little bro. I don't know how else to say it except I'm jealous sometimes, dude." He put his arms over the railing, leaning his forearms against the cold metal, and folded his hands, looking out over the ocean. We were both kind of too embarrassed to look at each other.

"I understand."

I understand? That was the best thing I could come up with after he'd just been man enough to apologize?

"Look," I tried again, "if it makes you feel any better, all this stuff gets me so scared that I constantly wish it wasn't me that had to . . . do it all, or whatever. I hate it sometimes, man."

"Really? It looks like you kind of enjoy being Superman to me."

"What do you mean? Am I getting cocky?"

"Well . . . kind of, I don't know. Just being honest, sorry."

"No, it's . . . it's okay. I'll try to quit being a poop head."

He swiveled toward me and shook his head.

"No, don't do anything different, I mean it. Geez, talk about stupid—it's about the dumbest thing in the world for me to worry about in the middle of all this garbage. You have to save the world, you little brat."

"Don't say that, it makes me feel like I can never do it. I'm just trying to tackle things one problem at a time. Right now, all I can think about is getting the last Gift. After that . . . we'll see what happens."

"Man, Jimmy, come on. Think about the things you can do. And didn't you say that old farmer guy told you the Fourth Gift is the most powerful or something like that?"

I nodded.

"Give me a break. What are you scared of? You're gonna kick some major tail when the time comes. And all of us— we'll be there, doing whatever we can to help. We're going to win, Jimmy, and get our old lives back—the good ole days, you'll see."

"I hope you're right, but it still scares the crud out of me."

"Well, ya know what? You may be my little brother, but I just want you to know that I look up to you."

He patted me on the shoulder, and walked away.

I was so glad he left then, because it would've really stunk for him to see the wet thing fall out of my eye.

CHAPTER 39

Not-So-Tender Moment

Two days later, I was sitting next to Dad, watching him as he continued his endless sleep. His chest rose and fell like normal, but he showed no other signs of life. It had been so long now, we'd kind of gotten used to it, but seeing him like that still ate at my insides. I just knew that everything would be a little better if Dad was up and about to lead us.

I didn't know what to do for him, but I tried to sit with him several times a day. In the back of my mind I hoped that he would wake up on my watch, because it would be so cool to go upstairs with him and show everyone who'd woken up.

Mom never tired in her efforts to clean and feed him—we left all that up to her. Sometimes when I watched her help him, she would check his pulse, look under his eyelids, listen to his heartbeat, and stuff like that. I thought I would do the same and see if I could figure out anything useful.

I put my ear to his chest and listened. *Bum-bump, bum-bump, bum-bump.* I put my two fingers here and there on his neck until I felt his pulse. I started to feel dumb, like I was trying to be a TV doctor or something.

I reached up to his right eye. I placed the edge of my thumb on his eyelid, and gently raised it up.

I yelled out in shock and stumbled off the bed onto the floor. My back crashed into a metal trash can, its edge digging into my spine. The sound of the can falling over and spilling its contents killed the silence like water on a flame.

I scrambled up and ran out the door, screaming for anyone who could hear me.

No one was around down in the cabin area. I shot up the stairs and stumbled through the door, frantic and wild.

"Mom! Joseph! Rayna!" I was yelling and running around like I'd finally lost it in the head.

Everyone had been chit-chatting in the lounge chairs, but they all sprang up and ran toward me.

"Jimmy," Mom said, her eyes afire, "what's wrong?"

"Dad! It's Dad!"

Joseph grabbed me by the shoulders, trying his best to calm me.

"What is it, Jimmy?"

I just could not make the panic subside, and found it hard to breathe.

"Dad . . . Dad . . . his eyes . . . his eyes."

Joseph was already leading us toward the door downstairs. "What? What's wrong with his eyes?"

My next words were hampered by sobs.

"His eyes are completely black—pitch black."

The next thing I knew, Joseph was dragging Dad up the

stairs and out onto the deck, laying him on his back. He lifted both of Dad's eyelids, and everyone saw my words confirmed.

Black. His eyes were pockets of emptiness, sucking in and devouring all light.

"No, no, no . . ." Joseph groaned over and over as he shook my dad, slapped him, trying once again to wake him after days and days of such efforts. He pulled back Dad's sleeve, where the strange scratches were now healed but still visible. Branching out from the scars were the beginnings of spidery, black veins.

"No!" he screamed. "No!"

Mom was crying beside them, weeping like a lost child. The rest of us looked on in stunned silence, not quite grasping, or more accurately, not quite accepting what we were seeing. But the truth lay before us, cold and silent on the deck of the ship.

Dad was turning into a Shadow Ka.

CHAPTER 40

Two Buds

Joseph and I dragged Dad back down to his bed, and with a bizarre feeling of being out of place, I pulled the covers over him. My heart hung like a stone in my chest, and I had lost all feeling. Unlike my mom, I couldn't cry, but the anguish inside of me was no less than hers. Everything else, all the worry and anticipation of the future, the quest for the remaining Gift, the battle against the Ka and the Stompers—it all sunk to the bottom of my thoughts.

My dad was turning into a monster, and he could do nothing about it. We could do nothing about it. Any semblance of hope that had lifted within me was now gone, as sure as a feather in the midst of a hurricane.

Mom kept trying after I'd tucked Dad in, although we all knew it was useless. She shook him, poured water on his face, tried her best to talk to him without breaking down in sobs. I couldn't bear to watch, and stumbled into the Mess Hall, slumping into the closest chair. I then put my head in my arms and wallowed in despair.

A world without Dad suddenly didn't seem so important to save.

Joseph made Captain Tinkles double our efforts to reach Japan. After the initial shock wore off, we were able to compose ourselves enough to discuss any possibilities for helping my dad. But there was nothing we could do, and the truth of it hurt like never before. So it was decided that our only choice was to make it back to land, and find a doctor. Surely there was some physiological explanation for how the Shadow Ka stole a human life—and maybe a doctor could somehow cure my dad.

But it was only a flippant hope, something to keep us from going completely insane. If we threw our efforts into running the ship around the clock, and keeping the boat in good shape, there was less time to sit and groan and weep and whine.

In the movies, they always have that cheesy line about how things could not possibly get worse, and then it starts to rain or something. I can honestly say that looking at my dad, miserable and silent in his bed, you could never have convinced me that circumstances would worsen.

But one day before we reached Japan, two things happened that made us long for the good ole days when Dad only had black orbs in his eye sockets.

That morning I was helping Rayna clean the decks up above. It was baffling to me how quickly dirt and greenish grime could build up on the surfaces of the ship, but it was good to have something to do. Rusty was fascinated with driving the ship itself, and he mainly helped in that regard. The captain had really taken him under his wing, and kept telling us that one day Rusty would make a fine skipper. Everyone else found their own ways to help, and we had stayed very busy for several days, trying our best not to think of our ship as a Shadow Ka incubator.

I was on my knees, scrubbing a spot that was determined to remain filthy, when Mom burst through the door from the cabins below. The look on her face was all we needed.

Something was wrong—*more* wrong—with Dad.

"What is it, Mom?" I asked, even as I was running past her to go downstairs.

She turned and followed me down, with Rayna right behind us.

"His skin," she said, "his skin is . . . changing."

Her words made my stomach turn, and I knew what I was going to see before we even got there. I reached their room and moved through the open door. By that time, Joseph had noticed the commotion and joined us.

"What's wrong?" he asked, dreading the answer.

I ignored him and ran to Dad's side. Something was wrong with the skin on his face. I pulled back the covers, grabbed his right arm, and pulled up his sleeve.

"Turn the light on!" I yelled.

My fears were realized. It still hit me with a sickening punch.

A spider web of black lines infiltrated his skin like a night-marish tattoo. It was still faint, nowhere near what we had seen on the other Shadow Ka, but it had begun to spread over his whole body.

And then a thought of horror flashed in my mind. I didn't want to do it; I didn't want to see if I was right. But it had to be done, and even as I did it, I knew there was no way that I could be wrong.

With a grunt of effort, I pushed Dad over onto his side and felt around the back of his shirt, damp from sweat.

There were two large bumps on the upper middle part of his back.

They were not shoulder blades.

Dad already had eyes of black emptiness, was lost in an endless sleep, and had black lines invading his skin.

Now he was growing wings.

CHAPTER 41

Bad Time to Swim

The human being can only take so much pain and distress. When we saw that Dad's entire body was turning into a monster—that we were losing our own father, husband, and friend, something clicked, and we became numb to the increasing horrors. We left him there, transforming in his own bed, and went about our duties, knowing that there was nothing to do for him but reach land and hope and pray.

Every time the thought of what was happening to Dad crept into the hallways of my mind, I did everything I could to think about Japan, and the hope that some person, or some thing, or some miracle waited there that would heal my dad.

It would turn out there was such a beacon of hope awaiting us on the island for which we were headed. But if someone had frozen time, given me a pen full of endless ink, and provided a million sheets of paper, I could have never guessed what it would be.

But I'm getting ahead of myself. The day in which we discovered the budding wings on my dad was far from over.

"To think that one year ago," Joseph said as we stood at the railing, looking out at the wavy ocean, "I was working, living in the mountains of Utah, just beginning to enjoy life again and think that our troubles with the Union of Knights had finally come to an end." He sighed. "Now I'm on a big boat in the middle of the ocean with my best friend turning into a monster right below me."

"Our lives are definitely a little strange," I said.

A big wave splashed against the yacht below us, throwing a fine spray up to where we stood.

"Just imagine," Joseph said, "if we could go back to normal life, and snap our fingers so that none of this would have ever happened. We would never take anything about our ordinary, boring lives for granted, would we?"

I shook my head. Rayna walked up from behind and joined us.

"I hope that Geezer," she said with a slight tap on my shoulder, "as Jimmy here has so eloquently named him, has fulfilled his duty and gathered the Alliance—or at least as many as possible. We could use their help."

"How many are there?" I asked. "How many members of the Alliance?"

"There are many and there are few."

I let out a fake laugh. "That sounds just about right—like most of the answers I get to my questions. Yet another riddle."

"Jimmy, the day comes that you will know everything. Even after everything you know now, you are not ready for the entire truth. But when that day arrives, you will understand what I mean that there are many and there are few." She paused for a minute, and I couldn't think of anything to say to urge more out of her, and wondered if she was finished.

"But suffice it to say," she continued, finally, "that on this world, at this time, there are few, I am afraid."

"How many?"

"Ten and a half."

"Um, a half?"

"Yes, you will understand when you meet him. He is a Half."

I had some absurd vision in my head of a one-eyed, one-armed, one-legged man hopping in circles, and a giggle slipped out of my mouth.

"Don't laugh, Jimmy," Joseph said.

"What, do you know about this half-person?"

"Yes, I learned almost everything there is to know about the Alliance while in the Blackness. I have never met the Half, but I can't wait until I do."

"Well, whatever it is, nothing could top Tanaka on the weirdness scale."

Rayna surprised me when she laughed.

"Yes," she said through her chuckle, "Tanaka is the strangest of our lot— that I cannot argue." She sobered up and continued: "But he is the bravest, most compassionate man you will ever meet, Jimmy. I promise you that."

A noise from behind startled us. It was Tanaka, and the noise had been something bodily, which I didn't want to figure out.

"My lips are burning," he said. "Someone talk about me, neh?"

I looked into Tanaka's bushy hair-lined eyes, gazed at his greasy mane and scraggly beard, and felt the same admiration for him as Rayna. He was definitely a good man, despite, and sometimes because of, his quirkiness.

"Uh, Tanaka, old man," I said, "that's your ears that were burning, and yes, Rayna here was telling us about the time you lost to her in arm wrestling."

"What!" he roared. "Never!"

"Calm down, tiger, I'm just kidding. Where's Miyoko?"

"I'm right here." She was coming down the steps from the front part of the ship.

"So let's see," I said. "So far I know about Hood, Tanaka, Miyoko, Rayna, and Geezer. Oh, and the Half, whatever that is. That's six—I mean, five and a half. Who and where are the others?"

"You will meet them soon enough," Rayna said. "Geezer will have them gathered. By the way, his real name is George."

"Geezer's name is George? I think I did him a favor, then."

For some reason, at that moment I thought of chasing Geezer in the train with my dad, and the pain of what was happening downstairs returned. In order to ward it off, I quickly thought of something else.

"Tanaka," I asked, "when are you going to fess up and tell us what the deal is with the big monkey?"

"Big monkey?" he asked. "You talking about Jimmy-san, or do you mean the *okisaru?*"

"Funny. Seriously, what was that thing, and why did it touch you on the head?"

Tanaka did not answer, and our brief moment of levity evaporated like mist in the desert.

His eyes closed, and he sat down on the deck. Then he slumped over and collapsed onto his side.

"Father!" Miyoko yelled, running up to him.

A groan escaped from him as she shook him gently. Then his eyes popped open, full of alarm.

He jumped back to his feet, and looked around like a wild animal seeking its prey. His head darted back and forth, his eyes searching for something unknown to any of us.

"Tanaka, what's wrong with you?" Joseph asked.

"I must, I must, I must," Tanaka said over and over, looking about. He acted like we were not there, and that he had gone batty.

"Father, please," Miyoko said, trying to grab him and make him look at her. "Talk to me!"

Tanaka froze. He shook the cobwebs out of his mind, and then everything changed. The wildness, the lunacy, left him in an instant, and the old Tanaka—the normal crazy Tanaka—stood before us once again. He looked around, taking in each of us.

"I very sorry that it take me so long to realize what I must do."

He turned to Miyoko, and put his hand on her cheek.

"I love you, sweet daughter. You trust your father, neh?"

"What are you talking about? Of course I do—what is going on?"

"I cannot tell you now. Trust your father is all I say, neh?"

He turned and walked to me. "Jimmy-san, you are funny looking boy, and you throw up on me all the time. But I love you, and put my daughter in your care."

He stepped back, and once again took us all in his bushy-browed gaze.

"I go now, and prepare *okisaru* for the great battle."

We had no time to ask him what in the heck he meant.

I felt in my heart that a day would come when nothing could ever surprise me again. But what Tanaka did after uttering those strange words made my jaw drop and threw our thoughts into chaos.

He turned his back to us, walked up to the railing, and swung himself over the side into the ocean below.

By the time we ran after him and looked down into the watery depths, he was gone, swallowed by the sea. A crystalline swath of splash marked his point of entrance.

Tanaka had jumped into the ocean for no reason.

With a sick heart I watched and waited, but he did not resurface.

CHAPTER 42

The Wrinkled Stranger

I'll never forget the look of perfect sadness that graced Miyoko's face in the days after Tanaka jumped ship. Nothing could console her, and even though I had my own father turning into a hideous beast, I felt more sorry for her. She cried, and she drooped, and she wished the world to end. I felt guilty for having asked about the *okisaru* in the first place.

The night before we reached the coast of Japan, we had a little chat, and a faint sliver of hope seemed to swell within her once more.

"I've decided that my father is not dead, and not crazy," she said, breaking my thoughts away from the churning waters disappearing below us as the boat sped toward land. The fading sun sliced through the water, creating strange hues of all colors.

We'd already been through all of this. Not one of us could come up with even the slightest hint of an explanation for Tanaka's inexplicable dive into the biggest bathtub this side of Mars. Not one explanation—except for the saddest one of all. That he'd finally lost his last remnant of brain and went

191

berserk, jumping to a very unpleasant—and very wet—death.

"Miyoko," I said, "I don't even know what to say anymore. As much as it makes me want to puke, I think that we need to face the truth. How could your dad have possibly survived? No person could swim that far—it's impossible."

It sounded harsh, but every person on the ship had already had this conversation with Miyoko. Unless Tanaka had become personal friends with the captain of a nuclear submarine lately, there was just no way he was alive.

"You don't understand my father," she continued. "Because he does not speak your language very well, and because he is a bit zany sometimes, you think him irrational—a man of bad judgment. But let me tell you something."

She turned from the railing of the ship and faced me, her finger pointing right between my eyes, like the last gunslinger of the Old West.

"Not once in his entire life did my father make an unfounded or foolish decision. He was—is—the most intelligent and rational person I have ever known. I'm ashamed that I doubted him so much up until now." She dropped her hand and turned back toward the ocean. "As crazy as it seems, as unexplainable as it seems, I know that my father knew what he was doing. I know that he is alive."

"Well," I said, "whatever he is, dead or alive, swimming the backstroke or camping inside of a whale, I think he's better off than my dad."

And with that, I hurried off, pretending I had something to attend to.

Three hours later, Captain Tinkles came running around the yacht, screaming with glee.

"Ahoy, maties, dudes, and chicks! Land straight ahead! Land!"

That word, *land*, was like the sound of a trickling stream to a man lost in the desert. My heart lifted out of the heavy gloom of recent days, and before I knew it, I was singing. I was actually singing. It was a terrible song, with made-up lyrics and completely out of tune, but it was beautiful all the same.

As one, we scrambled to the front of the ship and leaned over the railing, staring with all of our might to catch sight of dirt, stone, and trees. Mom, Rusty, Joseph, Miyoko, Rayna, members of the crew. We were suddenly like kindergartners at the zoo, looking at the rhinoceros take a poop.

"I see a building!" yelled Joseph, as he twirled away from the railing, doing some bizarre dance while snapping his fingers.

"I see it, too!" said Miyoko, having lost all sense of her earlier mood. "There's another one—and I think I see some mountains behind them!"

Even Rayna, Miss Serious herself, made some goofy comment about wanting to squish mud between her toes, which made my stomach turn when I pictured it.

The faint horizon of buildings, mountains, and trees solidified as we stared, and before long, we knew we were almost there. *No Christmas morning has ever felt this good*, I thought, seeing solid land once again after so many weeks of bobbing on liquid.

The captain adjusted our course, and we headed for a long pier that jutted out hundreds of feet into a large bay, with several ships docked along its length. The day had been cloudy, wet, and cold, so there was no sign of activity anywhere along the wooden structure.

As we approached, I looked up. The skies had grown increasingly gloomy the closer we got to land, and it wasn't always explained by clouds. We'd discussed it several times, but no one had been able to explain it. But there was something wrong with the sky above us—it was becoming hazy and dark, even at midday when there were no clouds. But I couldn't see anything right then because of the storm.

"Oh, baby," Rusty said, snapping me out of my thoughts. "I'm gonna get down on my knees and lick the first patch of dirt I see."

"I thought Rayna's idea was disgusting, but you got her beat," I replied.

"All I want is a bed," Mom said, "A real bed, in an actual structure that doesn't move up and down."

Of course, through all of this, the thoughts of Dad and Tanaka lingered in the backs of our minds like body odor in a movie theater, but we allowed ourselves a moment of reverie.

The dock grew larger as we approached, and it became evident that not only was there little activity, the place looked like it had been completely deserted, as if a massive hurricane were approaching. No matter where we looked, we could see no sign of a living person.

Except one.

❧

A lone figure, stooped and withered, stood on the very end of the dock. He was leaning on a wooden cane, looking in our direction. His demeanor left little doubt that he was waiting for us, inexplicably expecting us.

My first thought was that maybe the person was Geezer, having fulfilled his duty to gather the remaining members of the Alliance—waiting to proudly tell us of his success. But as we slowed in anticipation of docking, I got a better look at him, and it was definitely not Geezer.

The man was ancient, the wear and tear of decades evident in his face and hands. He was dressed in tattered gray clothes, and the knobby cane he leaned on matched the look of the knuckles on his hands, arthritic and knotted. His face was almost featureless, lost in a sea of wrinkles and age spots. His hatless head revealed only slight remnants of what used to be hair—now only wispy trails of stringy cotton. He made no move as our massive ship pulled alongside the dock, directly next to where he stood.

He was in the same position twenty minutes later when Joseph, Miyoko, and I walked down the portable walkway from the yacht to the wooden platform of the dock. By then we had assumed he was a strange man who just wanted to spend his last days staring at the ocean—maybe waiting for his lost love to return from a tragic voyage.

We walked past him, intent on finding some local help to take care of the business of docking, unloading our luggage and supplies, and the like. We were only three or four feet beyond him when he spoke, stopping us with his words.

"Jimmy Fincher, we must talk."

His voice matched his age, a scratchy sound that struggled from his throat, like a radio station losing its signal. But his words were as powerful as thunder leading a storm.

"I am here to save your father."

CHAPTER 43

An Invitation from Evil

His last phrase had all the power of a brick wall, halting us with his cruel promise. It took a moment to formulate a response, but I was the first to speak from our group.

"My dad? How would you know anything about my dad?"

The old man twisted his frail body, moving his cane inch by inch, turning ever so slowly to face us. It was as if an ancient oak tree had finally tired of its resting place.

"My boy," he said, "your father is in the grasp of a fate you would not wish upon your fiercest foe. Your father is becoming."

"What do you mean, old one?" asked Miyoko.

"He is becoming. Soon there will be no return, and he will be one of them—no trace of his former self, fully in the service of beings so terrifying that your very bones will turn to mush just seeing them." He coughed, a hacking, wet explosion of noise. "Once the Shadow Ka call you one of their own, there is no escape to be spoken of."

The icy chill of his words seemed to freeze my heart.

"What did you mean when you said you had come to save my dad?" I asked.

"I meant what I said, boy. Only I know how to reverse this horror in which he is entrenched."

"And how do you know how to save him?" asked Joseph. "He's practically a full-blown Shadow Ka right now."

"How do I know?" He shifted even more weight onto his cane, the strain of it making an audible groan. If the pause that followed was for dramatic effect, it was completely unnecessary.

"Because I am one."

The man refused to speak any more, and handed over a slip of paper with Japanese writing scribbled all over it, presumably an address. We were instructed to meet him there that evening, after we'd settled in from our long voyage. I protested, frantic to find out what he was talking about, but he was insistent, waving his gnarled hands in definite refusal. Then he began a journey of his own, an arduous walk down the long wooden pier. We watched him for several minutes, in awe of his mysterious words.

Joseph then shouted to the man, an eruption in the silence.

"So, who are you anyway? Do you have a name?"

The old man halted his steps, and turned his withered head back in our direction. He answered in a scratchy whisper of a voice, only five words long, and at first my mind refused to believe I'd heard him correctly. But there was no mistaking what he'd said, and there was no way it could be a coincidence.

Sometimes, the entire world can change with a few vibrations of the vocal chords—just three or four spoken words. How many people have had their lives come crashing down around them with only a short sentence? "You have cancer," or, "He didn't make it," or, "You're fired." The answer that slipped through the old man's lips impacted me in every way as if someone had just taken an elephant and dropped him on my head, or reached inside of me and ripped my lungs out. His answer crumpled every hope he had offered with a vicious squeeze.

"What . . . did you say?" Joseph asked, his trembling voice reflecting the fear of what he knew he'd just heard.

The ancient man took a breath, shifted his body with a wince, and then looked up with yellowed eyes.

"I said my name is Custer Bleak."

With that, he turned and resumed his exodus to the shore.

CHAPTER 44

Odd Place to Meet

"How can we go? How can we *not* go?"

Joseph argued with my mom, who could barely stand when she'd heard the news that we'd met a man claiming to be Raspy, my fiercest enemy. It made no sense, since we'd seen him months ago already in the middle of his evolution into a full-blown Shadow Ka, and now he looked human—withered to the point of death, but human.

"What do you mean, Joseph?" she pled. "How can we willingly go to a place where that monster of a man has invited us? I don't care if you think he's not the same—I don't care if he's spouting off some nonsense about being 'healed' from the Shadow Ka. We meet enough danger as is without seeking it out ourselves."

My whole world was spinning. We'd spent a couple of hours in a dazed trance, unloading our belongings, finding a hotel, moving Dad with a blanket over him to hide his hideous state of being. His skin grew blacker by the hour, now, and the budding wings on his back were taking definite shape.

It sickened me to look at my own father, and hope was draining from an already empty tank.

And just when a glimmer of a chance had sparked before us, the name Custer Bleak had come back to haunt us. Now Mom and Joseph were having a heated debate on whether or not we should keep our appointment with Raspy, or Custer, or whoever he was.

"Listen," Joseph said softly, trying to calm my mother. "Listen to me. Your husband is on the verge of being the same kind of monster you just talked about. We should do anything, I mean *anything*, no matter how dangerous or how remote, to save him. If this guy is really Custer, then he has somehow ceased to be a Shadow Ka. I mean, how could he hide it?"

My mom could only shrug, not knowing what to say. She was just frightened for her family, for her husband—she was completely overwhelmed. I could see it in her eyes. Joseph continued.

"And if he's not Custer, or Raspy, or whatever we're calling him, then we have nothing to fear at all. Why he would make up such a thing, I don't have a clue. But my point is this: we have to go there tonight and see what that old coot has to say. We have no choice."

Mom began to cry.

"Come on, Mom," I said. "It'll be just fine. You keep forgetting that I have a few things up my sleeve. That old crusty guy won't be able to hurt me." I looked over at Joseph. "To be safe, maybe I should go alone."

Joseph shook his head like three hornets had just flown through his ears for some brain pie. "No way, boy, don't even think it. You and I are going, and that's that. I don't care if

I have to hold your hand the whole time so the Shield will protect me—I'm going."

And so it was settled. Rusty and I had a good talk, and even he agreed that Mom needed somebody to be with her, so he decided to not put up a fuss this time and stay. Of course, Rayna, Hood, and Miyoko were riled up to no end when they were told to stay, but we finally convinced them that more people would only complicate things.

It was decided that everyone would put their heads together and have another brainstorming session on finding the Northless Point while we went to our meeting.

Thirty minutes later, after a quick bite of Japanese fast-food (in which I swore I saw something wiggle just as I put it in my mouth), Joseph and I set off for our meeting with the very old man.

The air was cold and wet, and before long our clothes were damp and uncomfortable, even though it wasn't raining. We walked along a ways until we came to a busy intersection, and a long line of yellow taxis waited for our beck and call, like a giant metallic worm waiting to eat its next victim. Joseph being the adult and all, I let him figure out how to communicate with the taxi man, and soon we were zipping down the slick streets toward our destination.

Bright neon signs zoomed past as the Japanese man decided he wanted to impress the Americans with his uncanny driving abilities. Horns blared and incomprehensible insults from pedestrians seeped through the glass of the windows. Joseph looked over at me and we both burst out laughing at the same time.

"Hamburger French Fry, neh?" the driver said from in front. In the back, we exchanged puzzled glances.

"Uh, what's that?" Joseph asked.

"Coca Cola hot dog," he replied. "Harry Potter Britney Spears, neh?"

We weren't quite sure what he was talking about, so we stayed quiet and tried our darnedest to stifle our giggles. We failed something awful, and I'm sure the driver went home to tell his wife that the rude Americans didn't appreciate his amazing abilities with the English language.

After a few minutes of torturous efforts not to laugh, we arrived.

Joseph paid the driver, and we stepped out of the vehicle, telling him to wait for us. As the car idled, we turned and stared at the place in front of us. Joseph instinctively looked down at the piece of paper containing the address for our meeting. Of course, it was in Japanese, so we had no idea what it said. Miyoko had just told us it was an address and that the Taxi driver should know where it was located.

"Are we at the right place?" I asked.

"I guess so," Joseph said. "But I sure didn't expect this. We must not have been paying much attention during the drive."

We were standing in what appeared to be a large parking lot, empty of cars or anything else except for the taxi and the enormous object in front of us.

It was an airplane.

CHAPTER 45

Lifestyles of the Rich and Shadowed

It looked for all the world like Air Force One, that massive plane the President flies in, but I looked, and there were no words anywhere to be seen on the aircraft. It was beige, and very big—but nothing else to distinguish it or make it unique. A door was open on the side closest to us, with a large, portable staircase leading to it from the ground. The intent was clear. We were supposed to get on that plane.

"What do you think, Jimmy?" Joseph asked.

"What's there to think? Let's start climbing."

We walked the thirty or forty feet over to the plane, and as we did so, it became clear just how big the thing was. It towered over us, until it seemed it was the only thing we could see in all directions. When we made it to the foot of the staircase, I looked up. I remembered an old movie about an escalator that went to Heaven. It had seemed shorter than the steep mountain of stairs I was about to ascend.

I went first, with Joseph right behind me, step by step. The Shield could protect both of us, but Joseph had to be careful not to get too far away from me. Holding his hand would have actually been a good and safe idea, but neither one of us was going to be the first to suggest it, so it never materialized.

The steps were steep and hard, and we were only halfway when my calves began to ache. Step after step we climbed. I took a moment and peeked over the edge, and for a second I thought the plane had taken off with us attached. I couldn't believe how far away the ground was.

We made it to the open door, each trying to hide our heavy breathing from the other. I was going to say something, but realized it would give away how winded I was, so I just nodded my head, indicating I was going in. I stepped through the door into the plane.

A soft, warm heat enveloped us, and it was matched by the glowing, cozy feeling of the luxurious interior. Paneled wood and richly framed artwork covered the walls, and lush carpet supported our feet below. In front of us was a large room, bigger than any room in my own house, much less a flying aircraft.

Plush, leather couches and fancy high-backed chairs filled the room, with low tables scattered here and there. There was enough furniture to seat all of my cousins, and I had to look back through the open door to reassure myself that I didn't just step through some new kind of magic portal other than the Blackness. It seemed impossible that I was in the lap of luxury, inside an *airplane*.

We took it all in rather quickly and then noticed that we were not alone.

The man claiming to be my archenemy was sitting alone in a chair in the corner, his cane leaning against his knee, arms folded in his lap.

Custer Bleak. Raspy. Leader of the Shadow Ka.

It was almost indiscernible, but my heart skipped a beat when I realized that the man did indeed look like the Raspy I had met on several unfortunate occasions. He looked fifty or sixty years older, but I realized that it was him. He had looked old before. Now he looked *really* old.

But it was *him*.

He was sitting like a forlorn rest home occupant, awaiting his lonely death. He did not speak, but only stared with his cataract-laced eyes.

"We've come, just like you asked," I said. I took a breath, waiting for his reply. When I received none, I summoned the courage from deep within.

"Surely you know I've received three of the Four Gifts. You know there is nothing you can do to me. Why have you called us here? Why would you try and trick us by offering help for my dad—when it's you and your monsters that caused it in the first place?"

Nothing.

"WHY!" A sudden urge to blast him with the Ice filled me, and he still hadn't even said anything.

A wracking cough exploded from his wrinkled mouth, and it went on for several seconds before he settled and went still. Then, after an eternity, he spoke.

"It matters not to me if you have received one, two, three, or all of them, boy. You must know by now that the Fourth Gift is the only one that will matter in the end. It is the only one that can make a difference. So spare me your brave rantings."

His malicious words cleared the last cobwebs of uncertainty from the air, and there was no longer any doubt that Raspy sat before us.

"I don't get it," said Joseph. "What purpose could this possibly serve, this whole charade of luring us here, to another one of your fancy lairs?"

"I have reined in my true self for a time," he said. "I pulled my better existence inside until I was in a more manageable position to speak with you. You *people* cannot understand the exultant joy of being one with the Ka—or the pain and sacrifice of doing what I am doing. All just to speak with you."

"Stop the mumbo-jumbo, *please*," Joseph said, not trying to hide his disdain for the crusty old buzzard.

"Wise up, Joseph." The man spat his words, revealing his evil nature and increasing my alarm. "Do not think I have forgotten your deeds in this tale. If it were not for your cowardice, you could have had a life far beyond your meager and dull imagination."

Raspy stood, with a sudden change in his demeanor—faint but certain. A new strength filled him, and the cane dropped to the floor with a dull thud, no longer needed.

"Now listen to me, and no more petty word games. Jimmy, you have gone too far, and it is time to stop. I am prepared to make a deal with you, once, and then we will never speak again. There will be no bickering, no negotiation, no added terms. I will say this once, and you will give me your answer. Then you will leave my plane."

A heavy knot formed in my throat. Raspy's words filled me with a fear I had not felt in quite some time. It was not the fear of death or pain, but the fear of ultimate defeat and loss of all hope.

"What is the deal?" I asked, hanging on the silence that bridged the gap between my question and his reply.

"You must bring me the Red Disk, and I will save your father."

My blank stare was enough to show him I had no idea what he was talking about.

"You will bring me your father," he continued, "and you must bring him right away for it to work. Then follow the instructions given to you by the Givers. You do not know this, but you will obtain a relic called the Red Disk. It is the key to finding the Dream Warden, a title you have no doubt heard by now."

I nodded.

"When I have the Disk, your father will be returned to you, free forever from the Ka that grows within him, even now. You will bring me the Red Disk. I will save your father. Decide. Now."

"Forget it," Joseph said. "Forget it, Jimmy. Might as well call up the devil himself and make a deal. It'd be better than dealing with this thug. Come on." He grabbed my elbow and pulled me toward the door.

"Decide. NOW!" Raspy screamed, losing all remnants of the voice that had created the name I knew him by. "This is your last chance!"

"Blast him and be done with it, Jimmy," Joseph was furious. "Come on. Put an end to him once and for all."

The sea of emotion and thoughts within my head were in a tailspin, but I mentally slammed a door, and filled myself with calm. There was no time to think, no time to pick the pros and cons apart. I reached within, to the center of whatever it is that provides guidance and intuition, and I made my decision.

"We will return in one hour," I said. "With my dad."

Without another word, I turned to leave, Joseph joining

me—under protest. A sickly, demonic laugh trailed us all the way down the stairs, and only ceased when the taxi doors shut and we drove away.

I had the sickest feeling that I had just traded the world for my dad.

CHAPTER 46

Free Delivery

The next two hours were impossibly difficult. Joseph railed on me the whole drive back to the hotel, and then everyone else joined him when we reunited. Of course, Mom was the worst, almost delirious in her refusal to let me take Dad to Raspy. Weeping uncontrollably, she collapsed on him, holding him, swearing she would never let him go.

"Please, everyone, you must trust me!" Desperation fortified my voice. I reached down and grabbed Mom by the hand. "I can only use the Anything three more times, so if there is a way to heal Dad without using it, I mean to figure it out. If worse comes to worst, in the end, I will use it to save him. Trust me. How can it be any better to leave him here, developing more and more each day into . . . that." I pointed down at his moist, gray skin, cobwebs of black covering him everywhere, the budding wings tilting him to one side at an awkward angle.

Discussion ensued; argument and debate heated the room. But in the end, I won.

And so I ended up in the back of a taxi, sitting next to

a huddled mass hidden under a blanket, ready to deliver my own dad to the worst person I had ever known.

Our taxi driver said nothing about hamburgers or Britney Spears.

If I had thought it difficult walking up the portable staircase before, it was right near impossible dragging a two hundred pound man-beast up them. I held his legs and Joseph grabbed under his arms. We grunted and sweated and groaned, and thumped Dad's poor shadowy head on the steps more than once. Just before we were ready to call it quits and roll him back down the flight of stairs, we realized we were at the top.

Custer Bleak, otherwise known as Raspy, sat in the same chair, in the same corner.

"Put him on the couch." He had gained back his calm and old-manliness since we'd left, and I wondered how long before he let himself turn back into a full-fledged Shadow Ka.

We flopped Dad onto the soft leather, and then took a moment to catch our breath.

"You have to give us some collateral—something that will ensure your end of the bargain," Joseph said.

"I give you nothing," Raspy said, his wrinkled grin revealing yellowish green teeth.

"I promise you this, Raspy," I said, "If you fail to save my Dad, our whole world may lose in the end, but you will not be there to enjoy the victory."

His harrowing, cackling laugh echoed off the wooden walls. "Why do you insist on using that name with me boy?

Call me Custer Bleak, First Servant to the Stompers, and may you never forget it." He pointed a gnarled finger to the door. "Now be gone, and don't return until I see the Red Disk in your hands."

Disgusted, we turned to leave.

"One more thing," Raspy said. "Do not make the mistake of thinking I will order my Ka to leave you alone on your quest. They will still hunt you and do everything in their power to stop you. If they succeed, I win. If they fail, and you obtain the Disk and return, I win. Pretty good odds, don't you think?"

With no response, I ran down the stairs, not wanting to be in his presence for one more second. We got in the taxi and left.

❧

Back at the hotel, there was no helping the somber mood—the overwhelming gloom caused by recent events. Little was said, and every attempt at levity failed miserably. We retired for the evening in our respective rooms, thinking that our dreams could never be as bad as real life.

The next morning was dull and gray, no help at all to our dreary dispositions. We met for breakfast in the hotel restaurant and then reconvened in Mom's room, the bed strangely empty without my comatose Dad lying there, *becoming*.

"Now all we have to do is figure out where the stupid Northless Point is located," I said. "And how in the world I'm going to find the Lady and the Red Disk and the Dream Warden and whatever the heck else in fifty-six minutes."

It was obvious that everyone had grilled their brains

thinking about the mysterious clue while we'd been gone, but silence was my only answer. It lingered like a bad neighbor for several minutes.

Then Mom broke the spell: "Piece of cake."

"What?" I asked. "You think I can do everything I'm supposed to in fifty-six minutes?"

"No, no, that's not what I meant. I'm talking about the Giver's riddle—about the Northless Point. I think I beat Tanaka to the punch." She smiled. We all remembered Tanaka's insistence that he would be the one to figure it out. But the look in Mom's eyes said it all—she would be the one to claim victory in his absence.

"I know where it is."

CHAPTER 47

The Northless Point

"Are you sure?" Joseph asked.

She looked around the table at us.

"Well?" a few of us asked with impatience.

"Well," she said, "think about it. What does your first instinct tell you when you hear of a place where there is 'no north'?"

I thought about it again, not for the first time. Then: "It makes me think it's way in the south, so far south that you can't even remember that there ever was a north."

"Yeah," Rusty said, "I was thinking that, too."

"Well, good thing we're not relying on you two, then," Mom said, surprising us all with her sarcasm. "The only place in the world where there is *no north*, is way up north!"

"Huh?" Rusty said.

"Right," she continued. "If you go as far north as you can, then you can't go north anymore. So north ceases to exist."

We all stared at her, and then right before she said it, it clicked in my own brain.

"The North Pole."

After further discussion, we all agreed. It was just hard to accept at first because it seemed like it should be more difficult to figure out. But it made complete sense. If you stood on the North Pole, the only direction you can go is south. So no matter which way you pointed, there would be *no north*.

"Well," Miyoko said, "that was the easy part compared to actually getting there. Even if we were trained and had all the needed equipment, how in the world would we get there in time?"

The hum of the hotel's heater was her only answer.

"Well," I said, "we need to get a plane or something . . ."

"Jimmy, you don't just run to the airport and tell them you'd like a ride to the North Pole—we would need to hire experts who travel in that terrain for research or something."

She was right. I had worried so much about figuring out where the Northless Point was located, I didn't even think about the impossibility of getting there. Such a remote place was not easy to get to. What could we possibly do? A dark cloud frustration and helplessness began to creep back over our little group.

The feeling did not last long.

Hood, who had not said a word since we'd made it back from our meeting in town, slowly stood, drawing our attention. He threw his Bender Ring onto the bed. It spoke for itself.

Of course. The Bender Ring. Hood had the ability to travel anywhere in the world with a drop of his magical red hula-hoop. It was instantaneous, albeit a very mind numbing experience—I would never forget my one trip using it.

And it looked like I'd be doing it again.

Rusty questioned why we hadn't used the Bender Ring for other things, like getting to the Tower of Air. It was a good question, with an easy answer. For one thing, we'd wanted to stay together as a group up until now, and the ring could only transport two people at the most. But more important, Hood could only use the Ring if he knew an exact destination. We never really knew exactly where the Tower was located, just a general idea, so it never would have worked for that.

But you can't get a more exact location than the North Pole. It's one spot, and one spot only.

But just to be safe, Hood wanted to test it out. We grabbed a map of the world that was hanging on the wall of the hotel room, and pinpointed on the map the location of the North Pole. Hood indicated that was enough to make the Bender Ring function. We followed him outside into the open air behind the hotel, making sure no strangers were around, and watched as he performed his trick.

I had never seen this before, as I was in the middle of the Ring the only time I'd been around when it had been used. Hood stood a few feet from us, and held the Ring high above his head, holding it with two hands spread evenly apart. Then he let it go, the ring slipping from his hands and falling to the ground at his feet.

As the Ring fell, Hood disappeared along its path. If you could have taken a picture when it was halfway down, you would have seen Hood's bottom half below the Ring, and nothing but air above it. When the Ring finally hit the ground, there was no noise, and the Ring itself disappeared. There was no smoke, no circular, flaming brand where his feet had been. There was nothing.

When he returned just minutes later, the Ring appeared first, floating six feet in the air, parallel with the ground. Hood materialized as it fell—the opposite of what we'd seen earlier. His robe was covered in frosty ice particles, and we could tell he was shivering underneath.

He knelt down and painted on the nearby sidewalk, even though I was pretty sure the owners of the hotel wouldn't appreciate it very much.

"I MADE IT. THERE WAS EVEN A BIG STICK IN THE GROUND PROCLAIMING IT AS THE NORTH POLE. WE WILL BE READY WHEN THE TIME COMES."

We had only two days. There wasn't much I could do to prepare for my trip into the Blackness, because I had no idea what to expect. But Mom solving the riddle of the Northless Point had given us a much-needed boon, and everything seemed to switch in an instant from dark to light. There was a palpable feeling of big things to come, just on the horizon. We felt rejuvenated.

The beginning of the end was near.

CHAPTER 48

Late Night Television

There were things to get done, decisions to be made before the appointed time of the Ripping of the Black Curtain up at the North Pole. Rayna and Miyoko decided to go and find Geezer, who had been directed to gather the remaining members of the Alliance. Because we'd returned to the very port from which we had left, and because so much time had passed since our departure, it was troubling that there was no sign of Rayna's friends.

Mom, Joseph, and Rusty would move to another hotel in the middle of the night, doing everything possible to keep their identity and location a secret, even though it appeared Raspy had an uncanny ability to know about our comings and goings. We were baffled how he had just happened to be waiting for us at the dock the day before. The Shadow Ka were watching, and it would be very nerve-wracking to leave my family again.

But I had to.

Hood and I would remain at the original hotel until we went north, as would Rayna and Miyoko until they left. We hoped that all the movement would cause some major confusion to the Ka if they were indeed nearby.

In the early evening before the Big Day, Rayna and Miyoko prepared their things and readied to set out on their search for Geezer. Mom, Joseph, and Rusty had left the night before under cover of darkness, calling us every few hours to let us know they were okay. My good-bye to them had been difficult, but it was not enough to dampen the renewed encouragement we all felt. Our final piece of the plan was that as soon as Hood and I returned from the north, we would all rendezvous at the place where we had left our horses when we departed on the ocean voyage.

I couldn't wait to see Baka again. I kept thinking to myself over and over that the next time I brushed down my horse, it would mean that I'd been to the Blackness and back. That I had been reunited with a healed Dad, and that we would all be back together again, ready to help the Givers in whatever way we could, even if I had lost my opportunity to obtain the Fourth Gift in order to save Dad.

I just wished I could skip ahead twenty-four hours and have it all be over.

I had a quick dinner with Rayna and Miyoko in the restaurant before they left, with little conversation. Our minds were on the tasks that lay ahead. When we'd given up on trying to build an appetite, Rayna said it was time for good-byes again.

"Once again," Rayna said, "we will scatter like we did when you fought the Bosu Zoku. Hopefully we will reunite under the same positive circumstances. Victory."

"Ah, it'll all work out just fine," I said. Everyone knew I was trying a little too hard to be positive.

"You keep telling yourself that," said Miyoko. "Don't make me have to come and rescue you. I've got my own things to take care of, okay?"

"Yeah, right, I'll do my best. If . . . *when* you find Geezer, ask him to take a bath, would ya?"

We exchanged hugs between the three of us, and they got ready to leave.

"Go back to your room and make sure Hood isn't watching scary movies. He gets nightmares." Hood never came to the restaurant, and avoided public places as best he could, so he was back in his room, doing who knows what. Can a man watch TV with a piece of cloth covering his face? I made a note to test that when I got back to the room, just for curiosity's sake.

"All right. You guys be careful, and hurry back. We'll go to the horse barn every day at five o'clock, looking for your return."

Since we'd learned by now that there are no words to say in such situations, we finally gave up and just said good-bye. I watched them walk out the door, finished off my water, and walked back to Hood's room. I had no idea what it would be like to share a room with a guy who lives in a robe and talks with his finger, and I would never find out. He'd insisted on having his own room. But we did exchange keys in case of an emergency.

Turns out he wasn't watching TV at all, but was snoozing on his bed, snoring like a stuffy nosed rhino. Despite the nervous feeling in my gut, I laughed out loud. For some reason, I just didn't think a guy who couldn't talk would be able to snore. I sneaked out and headed for my room.

I got ready for bed, although I had no idea how I could

possibly fall asleep. I turned off the lights, flopped onto my bed, and lay in the darkness, trying my best not to think of the coming day.

North Pole.
The Lady of the Storm.
Red Disk.
The Dream Warden.
Bargaining for my dad's life.
Custer "Raspy" Bleak.

The thoughts danced and jiggled up and down all through my brain, no matter how hard I tried to empty my head. After an hour or so of tossing and turning, I sighed and decided to switch on the TV, hoping it would serve as a distraction and lull me to sleep.

I would regret doing so, because what I saw robbed me of any chance of falling asleep. Every channel had switched to some type of news program, with the glaring words "Breaking News" flashing at the bottom of the screen. It only took a few minutes to get the gist of it.

The world had fallen into complete chaos.

CHAPTER 49

My Ugly Mug

The images flashing across the TV screen would have been disturbing enough if they had only been part of a movie. Knowing that what I was watching was real—actually happening in the world as I sat on the bed and stared—made my bones shiver.

No single phrase could sum up what I saw. But with each passing minute, I realized more and more that the terrible future predicted by both my enemies and my allies was here.

People running through the streets, screaming and looting, setting fires.

Frightened men and women cowering on the ground, hands over their ears, spooked by some unseen force.

Armies and Navies being readied for full alert status.

Airplanes crashing into the ocean, ships sinking out at sea.

Traffic jams, vehicle pile-ups, burning bridges, people abandoning their cars, buildings engulfed in flame.

But none of these things were the real news. They were only the reaction of a population that had finally learned the truth—the world was not the same one they had taken for granted for so many years.

Shadow Ka were everywhere. New York City. Los Angeles. Hong Kong. Sydney. Rio de Janeiro. Mexico City. Tokyo.

Tokyo. The capital city of Japan. They were close to us, even now.

Their evolution had progressed to an alarming state. Very few cameramen were brave enough to keep shooting when one came into view, but there were enough shots to see that almost no human characteristics remained. Black, winged shapes swooped through the cities, screaming their familiar call. The frantic masses had nowhere to run as they learned the harsh truth that the world had changed forever.

Then I noticed perhaps the most frightening thing of all. In almost all of the shots, difficult to see at first amongst the chaos, there were people . . . sleeping. The news commentators kept saying they were dead, but something told me they were wrong. I could possibly be the only person on Earth who understood that the Ka had no intent whatsoever to kill anyone. Thanks to Farmer and his lecture during my trip to the Tower of Air, I now knew what the Ka were doing.

Their demented mixture of fear and magic would lull us all into a special state of slumber, readying us for the onslaught of the Stompers—that formidable enemy that literally took the shape of our worst nightmares.

The Ka had begun their enormous task—preparing my world for the Stompers.

No wonder everything around us was like a ghost town—this had to have been going on for at least a few days. Things had progressed at an exponential rate while we were at sea, and like a ballistic missile to the center of my chest, I realized that our time was now up.

The Stompers were here. Any day now, the rest would arrive in full force.

A few minutes later, I couldn't take it anymore. With every new city, it was only more of the same. Chaos bred by fear of storybook monsters.

I grabbed the remote. Just as my finger pressed the on/off button, something caught my attention in the instant before the screen went dark. At first, I interpreted it as a trick of the mind—an effect of my exhaustion and stress. But I turned the TV back on anyway. The screen flared to life, and it instantly confirmed what I had seen.

I dropped the remote.

Spread across the TV, on worldwide television, a face stared at me that I had seen probably a million times during my short life.

It was me.

CHAPTER 50

Wanted: Jimmy Fincher

I'm sure my chin had dropped enough to make me look like a yawning baboon. I wouldn't have been more surprised if Hood had stood up and started singing *Supercalifragilisticexpialidocious* . . .

As still as a box of frozen fish sticks, I listened to the newswoman and her British accent.

" . . . the growing rumor that began in a small Japanese village has suddenly sparked perhaps the most urgent task of a generation. World leaders in an emergency phone conference immediately agreed to commission a joint task force for the sole purpose of finding the boy.

"Although stories of the young man known as Jimmy Fincher were hard to swallow at first—despite the vast amount of amateur video footage taken during the now-famous helicopter incident—it now appears to be shockingly true. Most applicable to our current crisis are the accounts of Fincher single-handedly defeating creatures similar to the ones that are now attacking the world in a vicious, synchronized assault, leaving countless bodies in their wake.

"It is widely agreed that the boy must have invaluable knowledge concerning the creatures and their purposes, not to mention the inexplicable and other-worldly powers he exhibited in defeating them in the oft mentioned and constantly debated incident spoken of previously.

"We at the BBC join our fellow news associates around the world in pleading for information that may assist the authorities in finding this boy, Jimmy Fincher. If you have knowledge that may lead to his whereabouts, please call the number at the bottom of your screen. Now, we are getting reports that new attacks have been caught on film in the southern portion of South Africa . . ."

This time when I turned off the TV, the black claws of a Shadow Ka were the last things I saw on the screen before darkness swallowed the room.

I rolled over onto my bed, grabbed a pillow, and stuffed it under my head. I knew sleep would not come, but I tried to clear my mind of everything to at least give my head a break. Of course, it didn't work.

Everything depended on tomorrow. I could call the number and tell them where I was located, but what good would it do? They'd probably send an entire army to whisk me away to some underground military base for questioning.

No. Make it to tomorrow, go to the North Pole with Hood, and find the Lady and the Red Disk. Somehow I would figure out a way to save Dad without jeopardizing my search for the Dream Warden, and then I would get the final Gift needed to defeat the Stompers. Then I could tell the authorities.

Just make it to tomorrow.

The dull glow of pre-dawn snapped me out of that strange realm between sleep and wakefulness. Never having fallen into a truly deep slumber, I had nevertheless drifted off into some sort of bizarre daydream world in which I kept imagining Tanaka coming back to us dressed in a tutu. As strange as it was, I rose from my bed with a renewed sadness for our lost companion.

These thoughts and feelings dissolved into oblivion as I remembered the news program from just hours earlier. The world was looking for me. The whole premise seemed more unlikely than the vision of Tanaka in a pink dancing outfit, returning from the depths of the ocean. But it was true.

The world was looking for me. They knew about the Gifts, they wanted my help. And I was about to run from them.

As I went to the bathroom for a quick shower, the images of thousands of people, lying in the streets as if dead, filled my head. How many people out there were mourning the loss of loved ones? How long was it taking for people to realize they were actually entrapped in a magical sleep? I was tempted to call the number flashed a million times on the screen by the BBC just to make sure the people knew what was happening—that the Stompers were really and truly coming now.

But the idea washed away with the rest of the sweat and grime as I showered. I had to focus. All that mattered for the moment was getting to the North Pole and entering the Blackness.

When I was dressed and ready for the big day, I called Hood's room. He picked up the receiver, without a word of course—they still haven't invented phones that transmit finger paint—and I told him it was time. I put on my backpack—to store the Red Disk and whatever else I might find—and looked down at the special watch we'd bought the day before in a little convenience store. According to the digital timepiece, we had an hour before the Rip opened. Then I would utilize the stopwatch feature to count down the fifty-six minutes once it did.

Fifty-six minutes. I had to enter the Blackness, find a gateway, enter a world full of waiting Shadow Ka without them noticing, seek out the Lady of the Storm, and follow her bidding in fifty-six minutes. Even Farmer had sounded less than hopeful it could be accomplished.

While I waited for Hood, it was tempting to turn the TV back on and see if anything new had developed. But it would be too distracting, and it was time to get down to business.

There was a sharp knock at the door. I took a deep breath and readied myself for the trip of a lifetime. I walked over to the door, grabbed the handle, turned and pulled. I looked out at the person who had knocked.

It was not Hood.

CHAPTER 51

Presidential Escort

"Mr. Fincher?"

The man standing in the hallway of the hotel was American and very large. He wore a dark suit with a red tie, and I was surprised that he had no sunglasses perched on his nose. Everything else about him yelled out three letters—

F . . . B . . . I.

A sense of panic swelled up inside of me.

"Yeah, I'm Jimmy Fincher," I said. I couldn't help but try and look around him for any sign of Hood, and the man noticed.

"Don't worry, Mr. Fincher, I am alone. My name is Hammer, and I'm with the Secret Service of the United States of America. I'm here to rescue you and your family and take you back home."

It seems like such a cliché, but the guy's words rendered me speechless. Of all the things to happen right before we left for the North Pole—after weeks of waiting for that very moment! I should've known from the TV report that they would find me in no time—I'd seen enough movies to know they were fast.

"Secret Service?" I asked. "I thought you guys protected the President."

"That's exactly what we're trying to do." The man (had he really referred to himself as Hammer?) reached out and grabbed my arm. "Please, come with me, you will be safe now. Where are your other family members?" He looked over my shoulder into the dark room and then focused back on me.

"They . . . uh . . . I don't know."

I didn't know what to do. Where was Hood? We had to hurry and get up there, time was running out. Hammer pulled me out into the hallway and told me to stay put. I looked in both directions, desperate for a glimpse of Hood. Where was he?

The agent searched my room and then came back. It was then I realized that he trusted me and had no reason to believe I wouldn't take him up on the offer to go back to America with all the protection of the United States Secret Service. They had no idea what I was up to and the things I had seen and done.

Whatever the case, there was one thing for sure—there was no way I could mingle with this guy any longer.

Without a word to him, I took off running down the hall.

Hammer didn't even bother shouting. He ran after me with a pounding of footsteps, all signs of his polite demeanor vanishing as he realized I wasn't so desperate to go with him after all.

My head start had been woefully short, so he was on me in no time. His hand landed on my right shoulder, squeezing me with the intent to spin me around. I dove for the floor and rolled, the Shield finally kicking in. His body flung over me, the look of surprise on his face a brief flash before he looked down to break his fall.

I scrambled to my feet and ran in the other direction. This time he did yell out.

"What are you doing? I'm here to help you!"

I didn't look back, hoping I'd gained a few more seconds. At the end of the hallway was a door that led outside, to a flight of stairs skirting the side of the building facing the ocean. I slammed into the door and it flew open. My whole body banged into the iron railing, and then I flew down the stairs, leaping and banging with reckless abandon, in the full clutches of desperation. My room had only been on the fourth floor, and I reached the ground just as Hammer erupted from the building upstairs.

"Fincher!" he yelled. "Wait! Please!"

I was already running to the front of the building. A quick glance at my watch revealed that the Rip would open in thirty minutes. Everything was crashing down—I had to find Hood or it was all a waste. He was my only means of getting there in time.

A person who thought well under pressure would've realized that the front of the hotel was the worst place to go—Agent Hammer's associates would surely be there waiting. I wasn't used to running from government officials. As I whipped around the corner of the building and headed for the front entrance, my mistake became evident. Five or six Hammer look-alikes waited there—one even had the typical mirror-lens sunglasses on, despite the complete lack of sunshine for as long as I could remember.

I came to a halt. Trapped. Running away from the building would do no good, because finding Hood was the only reason for losing these guys in the first place. Without Hood, there was nothing to run for.

One of the agents, a woman, sensed my defeat and walked over to a white van. She opened the double doors on the back, swinging them both outward until the inside was fully revealed.

Hood sat there, his head drooping even more than usual.

CHAPTER 52

Escape from the Good Guys

Hammer caught up from behind.

"Jimmy," he said, panting. "What's the deal? We're here to help you, man." I turned to face him, and he had his hands on his knees, catching his breath. "Come on, now, let's get in the van and get out of here."

My mind clicked into overdrive, trying to devise a plan. All we needed was the Bender Ring and ten seconds alone. Dejected, I walked over to the back of the van before an agent decided to grab my arm again.

Then it hit me that I was intentionally refraining from using my Gifts. For some reason it seemed strange to use them against these guys because they were good. I had never done that before, and realized that maybe that was why the Shield had seemed to take longer than usual to protect me from Hammer upstairs when he grabbed me from behind.

I looked at my watch. There was no more time to mess around.

"Uh . . . look guys, I really appreciate you coming to rescue us," I said, wanting to lessen the blow of what I was about to do, but not knowing how. "I can explain everything to you and to whoever else later, but right now my strange-looking friend and I have important things to do."

The agents looked at each other, asking with their eyes if I had gone nutso.

"Look, I don't know what to say. See ya, take care."

I stepped to the van, reached in, and grabbed Hood's arm. Our troubles were over.

Hood understood, and stepped out of the van, making sure he did nothing to make me lose my grip. Then everything went crazy.

Hammer was the first one to try and grab us. When his hand rebounded off of the Shield, the look on his face reminded me of the time my friend poured chocolate milk down Bonnie Bingle's back during lunch. When Bonnie gasped and whipped around, it turned out Bonnie was actually Mrs. Shaw, our homeroom teacher. My friend's face couldn't have shown more shock if it had been Homer Simpson whose shirt he'd just defiled.

As they always do, Hammer tried again, this time with more force. When the Shield threw him backward, the rest of the agents swarmed in. One by one, they flew in every direction, tumbling across the pavement.

Hood and I walked calmly to the hotel entrance, my hand firmly planted on his arm.

Once inside, we abandoned all sense of being cool and darted for the elevator. The agents ran inside just as the elevator opened with a soft "bing." We stepped onto the lift and turned, facing our annoying heroes.

They ran for us as one. Hood's pale hand reached out and hit the button for the third floor, where his room was located.

The doors began to close. The woman agent was almost on us. The sliding doors came to within a foot of closing when her hand reached through and set off the sensors, making the doors open up again.

"Please, lady," I said, "you don't understand what it is we have to do. Just leave us alone."

By this time, she stood there, holding the doors open, while the other agents joined her.

"Mr. Fincher," she said, "the whole world has fallen into chaos, and we know that you had something to do with it. One way or another, you are coming with us."

I hated to do it, but I had no choice.

"No," I said, "I'm not."

Trying to be as gentle as possible, I called upon the Ice. Misty swirls of air flew in from all directions, and encircled each agent with solid ropes of frosty Ice. More and more I called out of the air, wrapping them until they couldn't move a muscle. Surprising me, their looks went beyond even that of my poor friend when he poured chocolate milk on Bonnie-Bingle-Who-Wasn't-Bonnie-Bingle.

"Sorry," was all I could say.

A last burst of Ice pulled the female agent's hand away from the elevator, and the doors slid shut with a dull thud. The elevator began its ascent.

❦

We reached the third floor, the doors opened, and we sprinted to Hood's room. From some unimaginable place within his robes, he pulled out his credit-card key, and opened the door. We walked inside. Hood went over to the closet and opened it with his pasty hand. Inside, leaning against the back wall, was a vehicle faster than any space ship conceived by the most brilliant of scientists.

The Bender Ring.

Then the worst thing that can happen to a kid who is in a hurry to save the world happened.

I had to use the bathroom.

"Okay, Hood," I said, "hold tight while I use the bathroom. There ain't no way you're going in there with me." The thought hit me that I had never noticed Hood leave to use the bathroom since I'd met him, but it seemed the wrong time to ask him about it.

I went in to take care of business, hoping the agents didn't break out of the Ice and find our room in those few moments. Although my mom probably would've forgiven me under the circumstances, I paused out of instinct to wash my hands when my task was complete.

Just as I turned the water off and grabbed a towel, I heard the door to our room crash open.

With wet hands, I ripped open the bathroom door and ran out into the room. Three agents, different from the ones I had frozen with icy ropes, were holding Hood by the arms, his struggles useless against their strength. One of them spoke.

"Just wait, Jimmy," he said. "Please hear us out—we're only here to help you, to ask you to help us. We're out of options, and have no idea what is happening to our world. The skies are dark, mythical beasts are everywhere; people are falling into comas at an increasing pace. Please, help us."

The desperation in the man's voice was crystal clear, and pity filled my gut. But time was out, and the Rip would open any minute, thousands of miles away.

Saying nothing, I walked up to the group and grabbed Hood by the arm. They tried to stop me, but it was useless, and the agents couldn't hide their surprise at finding out their comrades had not been lying about the invisible Shield.

I smacked a ball of Ice against the agents' chests, and they tumbled backward as one, falling over each other with shouts of anger. I reached into the closet, pulled out the Bender Ring, and handed it to Hood.

"Let's go," I said.

Hood nodded, his droopy robe flopping up and down. As I held onto his arm, he raised the Ring above our heads so that we both stood within its circumference.

"Stop, or I'll shoot!" one of the agents screamed. "I swear to you, I *will* shoot!"

"Go ahead," I said, making sure I was touching Hood.

I had called the man's bluff, and he lowered his outstretched arm holding the gun, giving up.

Then Hood dropped the Ring. I caught a last glimpse of the agents as the Ring passed my eyes, a red swath of chaos following in its path, replacing the room around us.

We were on our way to the North Pole. I couldn't help but wonder if we had a better chance of seeing Santa Claus than seeing a Rip in the Black Curtain.

CHAPTER 53

No Sign of Elves

The racing, squiggly red lines seemed so familiar, even though it was only the second time I had journeyed with the Ring. They trailed the circle as it fell, seeming to devour the hotel room around us and replace it with demented, dancing lines on top of blackness. I followed the path of the falling Ring, and when it hit the ground, I stared at the circle of carpet, wanting to catch the moment of transformation.

Dizziness and nausea attacked me, but I focused on the ground. There was a flash of red across the carpet, like a flashlight shone through a red bed sheet. Then it faded into a bright light, the red quickly replaced by blinding whiteness. I expected the white to fade as well, remembering the time we went from the riverside to the yard outside of Tanaka's house, and seeing the green grass at my feet.

But the whiteness stayed, and the Bender Ring began to ascend, this time reversing its earlier course, devouring the disappearing red lines in its path, and leaving a trail of reality in its wake. Then it hit me. Of course. The whiteness.

How many movies about Santa did I have to see to

remember that the North Pole would be nothing but ice and snow? As the Ring moved upward, past my knees, past my waist, past my chest, there was nothing but blinding whiteness, glaring—the pure absence of color in all directions. Cold air washed through my clothes, a wetness in it that was like small needles prickling against my skin.

Squinting my eyes to shield the glare, I looked up. It was finished, and Hood was once again grasping the Ring with both hands above us. He pulled it over and down and let it fall to rest by his side. He pointed to our right.

I looked over, and willed my eyes to hurry and adjust to the surrounding light. The sky here was not dark like where we had come from, and the sun beat down upon the snowy landscape with unforgiving brilliance. Through the eyelash veil of my squinting eyes, I could just make out a vertical object packed into the snow, and walked over to it.

It was a thick, red post, with a white line spiraling down its length, just like a candy cane. A square sign was attached about halfway down, with several languages written on it in faded gold stamping. I scanned it for something recognizable, and found some English. It was so simple it sent shivers down my spine.

THE NORTH POLE

Known to some people, particularly certain god-like people from another world, as *The Northless Point*.

Hood acted like he wanted to tell me something, but seeing as we were in a sea of white, and his finger only talked in one color, he shrugged his shoulders and gave up.

"Are you okay?" I asked. "If I'm in there for fifty-six minutes, you'll get awfully cold. I know that robe is thick, but . . ."

He wagged his hand in the air, indicating it was nothing for me to worry about.

"If I'm not back in that amount of time, you might as well head back without me, okay? I guess your clue will be when the Ripping closes, right? Promise me you'll head back then."

Hood nodded. I had expected him to resist at least a little bit, but then remembered that the Shield was probably protecting me from the cold already, and that Hood was maybe already approaching the point of misery. I hoped he could handle an hour.

"Well," I said, "If you get too cold, head back for a while and then come back."

I looked around, and there was nothing but the same in all directions, from where we stood to the distant horizons. Flat, white land. No fat guys in red pajamas, no bustling toy workshops, no elves. A few years earlier I would've been devastated.

I looked at my watch. The Ripping was supposed to open in less than five minutes. Since my conversation with Hood was as wordless as a tongueless mute drifting in space, my mind wandered.

There was so much confusion, so much fear, so much pain. The turmoil of putting my dad's life above my duty to save the world from the Stompers gnawed at me, and I had the sickening feeling that I'd made an irreversible mistake. What good was Dad's life if it was spent in a world full of literal nightmares?

Somehow I had to right things. Who cared that I had

technically given my word to the monster named Custer Bleak? A deal with the devil is never valid. Somehow, some-way, I would figure out a way to keep the Red Disk out of Raspy's hands, and still save my dad. My decision on that matter was made, and I felt a lot better.

Of course, it was funny that I didn't even know the first thing about the Red Disk or why Raspy wanted it so badly. But the fact alone that he wanted it was enough to tell me it must be rooted in evil. Or that it was so important to our cause that he merely wanted to prevent me from having it.

Once again, I got fed up with my thoughts, and I pushed them away. Thinking too much could be really depressing sometimes. The Ripping of the Black Curtain saved me from any further mopey contemplating.

Later, when I thought back on the moment when the ripping, crackling sound first trickled through the frosty air, right on time, I realized that I never really doubted it would happen, not once.

Even as the blacker than black ink spot tore open in front of me, I reached down and set my stopwatch to 56:00, set to count down backward.

With a sense of bravery that somewhat surprised me, I waved to Hood, pushed the start button on my watch, and stepped into the Blackness.

I was about to experience the longest "just-a-hair-short-of-an-hour" in my life.

CHAPTER 54

Into the Blackness

It was only my second trip into the mysterious gateway between worlds. Just like the time before, there was a brief moment of floating, surrounded by darkness, before the substance of the Blackness seemed to form around me, and light slowly dissolved away the dark. I was standing on a black path of marble, winding away like a ribbon both before and behind me until it disappeared on the horizon. On both sides of the path, a great sea of inky, pale liquid stretched out for as far as the eye could see, eventually swallowed in migrating bodies of mist. The sky was dark and grey, as if the storm of all eternity was about to break.

The Ripping through which I had come stayed open, revealing a blurred vision of my home world on its other side. *Stay open, little buddy*, I thought.

The Blackness looked exactly the same as the last time I'd been there—not a smidgen more inviting. Scanning all directions, I saw no sign of a Shadow Ka or any other visitor, but spotted a widening of the path about two hundred feet away. It had to be the gateway Farmer had told me about—the one leading to the Lady of the Storm. Knowing my time was dwindling with every passing thought, I ran in that direction.

Our world, Earth, was unique in that it did not have a portal to the Blackness, which is why it had gone hundreds or thousands of years without being discovered by the Ka and the Stompers. It was instead separated by the Black Curtain, although how it all worked I had no idea. All I knew was that you could enter or leave the Blackness from any spot as long as there was a Ripping.

I kept running. I was about halfway to the landing.

The air was wet, and my clothes seemed to absorb it and moisten with every step I took. The gently lapping ocean of liquid silver looked menacing, like it would swallow you whole if you even dared to stick a tippy toe in it. Then I remembered my first visit, when the attacking Shadow Ka bounced off the Shield and fell into the waters, screaming, never to be seen again. I shivered as I ran.

The landings that held the iron gateways were made of a different material, resembling sandstone. After my brief sprint, I made it to the one I was to go through, and looked in awe at its less than comely state. The stone was jagged and uneven, with great breaks running through it in all directions. On one side, a large pillar jutted toward the grey sky, tipping precariously at its top like it had been trying to escape gravity and finally gave up.

The horror of those few moments after blocking the Black Curtain rushed into my mind, and I realized that the devastation of it had spread throughout the entire Blackness. I couldn't help but wonder if alien creatures lived somewhere in this place, under the strange ocean, or in the air, or on islands unseen, and whether or not they had been harmed during that frightful event.

But it couldn't have been any other way. The blocking of the Curtain just may have bought us enough time to make it as far as we had. Otherwise, the Stompers would've already controlled all of our minds and dreams to the point of no return.

I stumbled over the uneven ground to the stack of iron rings that formed the barrel-shaped gateway to whatever world awaited me. What kind of place did a Lady of the Storm live in, anyway? As I looked over the upper edge of the rings, something clicked in my head.

The scratches on my dad's arm. Although very crude, they had looked like a series of the letter 'O' overlapping each other. It looked a lot like the iron gateway! The revelation was bizarre, and my mind wanted to explain it away as coincidence. But the longer I looked at the rings of the gateway, the more they reminded me of the image of the scratches. But what did it mean?

Puzzled, I looked down at my watch. Forty-seven minutes. My mouth dropped open—how could nine minutes have already passed? I could no longer afford to think or pause for anything.

I placed the palms of my hands on the uppermost ring of the gateway, pushed down, and swung my legs up and over into the middle of the barrel. I knew there was no magic word, no fancy waving of the hand—it just happened.

Several seconds passed, and just as I began to worry that it might not work, a blinding flash of light erupted from the bottom of the iron rings and shot upward. My eyes shut on instinct, and when they opened again, everything had changed.

I was in a world forged by aliens, and it was raining.

CHAPTER 55

Purple

On one of our first days in Japan, when everything was still hunky-dory, it had rained in a way I'd never seen before. Having grown up in Georgia, where thunderstorms and tornadoes were not uncommon, that was saying a lot. The rain had fallen in sheets, impossible in every way to make out individual drops. Within seconds the gutters and streets had filled, and luckily it stopped after only a few minutes.

The onslaught of falling water I now stood under was twice as bad.

It was nighttime in this new place, and the pelting rain again reminded me of standing under the waterfall at the local amusement park. Wiping my face was futile, and I was forced to squint and try my best to see through the cascading deluge. I looked down.

A glowing light was coming from somewhere. Just as I had been warned, the gateway on this side of the Blackness was fragile, perched atop a thin rod of glass or crystal, looking like it could break with the slightest tap. Farmer told me that if it did indeed shatter, there was no return—the gateway would be ruined. He also told me that Shadow Ka would be there, somewhere, waiting to destroy it. This was going to get tricky.

I took just a moment to make out anything else I could see, and a lump the size of Texas formed in my throat. An instant blaze of panic almost made me faint.

The crystal rod holding me up protruded from the tip of a giant pyramid, made of an eerie, pulsing material that glowed varying shades of purple. The falling rain washed down its four angled sides in flowing sheets, slick and smooth. It looked like a fancy display in a shopping mall. One of the downward sloping edges formed by two sides of the pyramid had steps cut into it, leading down into darkness.

My pyramid was not alone. In all directions, there were countless more, made of the same material and in varying sizes, rising to an assortment of heights. They were all connected to each other in a haphazard manner, creating a wild maze of sloping walls and sharp edges, with the same cut stairs leading here and there amongst them. The rain made it difficult to see, but it appeared as if I were in an entire city of pyramids, jumbled and massed together like a crowded city on an Italian mountainside.

But none of this caused the lump in my throat and the panic in my chest.

On every pyramid, perched at its pointed tip, sat a full-grown Shadow Ka, wings folded, awaiting my arrival.

The whole plan seemed doomed before it even began.

Time was ticking away, and I had no idea what to do. The Ka could not hurt me—that was not my concern. But if I left the gateway, they would instantly swarm in and destroy the crystal shaft, trapping me there forever. And I certainly had no time to seek out and freeze or destroy every Ka I could see—they seemed to stretch into the distance forever and ever.

I looked at my watch. Forty-two minutes.

My first thought was to use the Anything. Maybe it was my only choice. I could call upon it to protect the gateway from harm, no matter what happened. But to use another one of the four chances was so risky. Farmer said at least one would need to be saved for the very end, which would leave me with its power to use only once more before that time.

Thinking of Farmer made it all come together.

In the last seconds of our conversation under the Tower of Air, he had said the Shield would be the key. I knew he'd told me more than once that the First Gift had uses that I had not yet realized. Was there a way to leave the protective power of the Shield behind? Maybe if I cut off my hand and placed it on the gateway, so it could be touching me? Okay, that was stretching it.

I couldn't help but look at the watch again.

Forty minutes.

I decided to take a leap of faith. I would always have the Anything as the ultimate backup.

Wishing I were invisible, I clambered up onto the top of the iron rings and shifted my body around so I was facing them. With every bit of care, I tried to climb down the rings and onto the crystal shaft by hugging and releasing, squeezing with my feet and legs for any possible support. Somehow it worked, and it was only as I slid down the rod like a fireman on his pole that I remembered that I could've just jumped and the Shield would have protected me just fine.

When my feet touched the slick top of the fluorescent purple pyramid, they slipped down the side until my arms— wrapped around the crystal—stopped my fall when they reached the juncture of rod and stone. I stayed still, hugging the glass, waiting for any action from the Ka.

There was no sign of their trademark scream, no sound of flapping wings.

I shifted my feet, slipping and sliding, until I could maneuver them over to the stairs. Although wet, they seemed somewhat secure, and I carefully pushed away from the crystal rod and stood up. The rain continued to pour from the black sky.

The closest Shadow Ka was only forty feet away, sitting atop a pyramid, with its highest point still below where I stood. It made no movement that indicated it even noticed my existence. It was there, making typical movements of a living creature, breathing, shifting every once in a while—but it didn't even so much as glance in my direction.

I waved my arms back and forth. No reaction. I almost yelled out, just to see what would happen, but stopped short. Why push it?

I took several steps down, careful not to slip on the wet stone. I looked back at the Shadow Ka and then at the others. They were ignoring me completely.

Then it clicked.

Maybe, just maybe, the Shield was far more powerful than I could have even dreamed. It repelled bullets, it repelled snow, it repelled exploding helicopters. And in the most bizarre of circumstances, when it was truly needed to protect me, perhaps it repelled something even more fascinating. Sight. Vision. The ability of others to see me.

Yes, it made sense. I had even wished it in my mind.

The Shield was making me invisible.

CHAPTER 56

Sliding and Lightning

Encouraged and confident, I continued to make my way down the narrow steps. A few seconds later, I slipped.

Before I could grab anything with my hands, I was off the stairway completely, sliding down the steep, slick pyramid. Thirty of forty feet later, I came to a junction with another structure, and changed directions, now sliding down the crevice created by the joining of the two pyramids. Soon, another turn, and then another.

With the Shield protecting me, it was nothing but fun— the greatest water slide ever created.

I slipped and slid down several more turns before I finally reached the bottom, which ended at the edge of a vast plane of the same glowing material, stretching out before me to infinity, flat as a perfectly sliced piece of cheese.

I stood and looked back up at the towering maze of pyramids. High in the distance I could just make out some Shadow Ka, resting and waiting. They had no idea I was here.

I looked to the left and right and saw that the pyramids went on in both directions seemingly without end, but they all came to a stop along a straight line, leading to the flat plane. It was like a busy beachside, countless condos and tourist traps lined up, facing an ocean of purple.

I turned and faced the vast emptiness, my clothes sopping wet. The deluge continued, and for the first time, I saw lightning and heard thunder. The storm appeared to be worse out there, and the lightning illuminated the sky to such a degree that I could see the cloud formations. They were swirling around a single point, like a miniature hurricane—like it was a living, breathing entity.

A deafening crack of thunder erupted from the central point, and a thick, blinding streak of lightning bolted down and smashed into the ground, seeming to linger for several seconds. Then it was gone. I continued to stare in that direction.

The next series of flashes revealed something where the blistering lightning bolt had struck—something that had not been there before. It was impossible to tell exactly, but the glimpse of billowing white material, flowing in the wind and rain, had to be my signal.

I began walking toward it. Then I ran.

I didn't need to look at my watch to know that time was disappearing with a ruthless sense of indifference.

❧

As I drew nearer, the image of the Lady of the Storm solidified and took shape, despite the drenching rain that did its best to obscure my vision. Parts of her long dress flowed ten or twenty feet from her body, dancing in the wind. But the rain did not touch her.

Her hair was long and red, cascading strips of velvet reaching her back and beyond. It was not the typical auburn or orange of usual red hair—hers was the color of blood. Her face was pale and gentle, with eyes bluer than the clearest sky. If I had been a little older, I might've asked her to marry me right on the spot.

I pulled to a halt about twenty feet in front of her and then walked with careful steps the rest of the way. A bubble of protection from the storm surrounded her, and I walked through it. Not only did the torrent of water end in an instant, but the sounds of the raging storm dissolved away as well. The sudden lack of rain made me wonder why the Shield had not been acting like an umbrella for me all that time, and I figured it had been doing me no harm—unlike the bitter snow and cold of the frozen world I'd visited my first time to the Blackness.

I stopped just a few steps short of the Lady, and waited for her to speak. Every instinct told me that she had expected me for some time now, and was ready to deliver whatever I needed.

"Hello, young Jimmy," she said, her voice crisp and pure, like the trickling runoff from the North Georgia mountains after a downpour. "Welcome to the Storm World, where things are very different from yours."

It was the understatement of the day, but I just nodded.

"You have obtained the Three Gifts, and seek the Fourth, am I right?"

"Yes," I said.

"You must know by now that I do not have this Gift for you, yes?"

My heart sunk a little, because I'd hoped that maybe this time it would be easy. But everything I had been told should have led me to believe that the Lady was only going to give me direction on how to find the final Gift.

"Right," I said.

"The final door you must open is not like the others, Jimmy. But it is a door nonetheless." Her eyes dropped, and she paused, as if in deep thought. I scratched my head trying to make sense of her last sentence.

"I give unto you the Red Disk." She reached into the folds of her flowing gown and brought out a flat circular disk, about the width of a typical Frisbee, an inch thick, and as red as the fiery hair flowing off of the Lady's head. She held it out, and I accepted her odd gift to me.

It was heavier than it looked, and very solid, like a piece of hard granite. I flipped it over and scanned both sides, but there was no break in its design. Red all over, with no blemishes, bumps, or lines. Smooth and cool to the touch.

Red Disk was as good a name as any, albeit unimaginative. I placed it in my backpack, and strapped it on a little tighter, just to be safe.

She continued her instructions.

"You cannot obtain the Fourth Gift until you have found the Dream Warden, who will then reveal it unto you. You cannot find the Dream Warden without the Red Disk, so I have done my part in giving it to you. But then, here is the difficult part."

Her face grew somber, and I didn't like that one bit.

"It is difficult to understand the Disk, for there is only one way to know how to use it."

"Only one?"

"Yes. The one called Erifani Tup."

"Erifanawho?" I asked.

"Erifani Tup. It is an unusual name, to be sure. But you must find and understand it, and you will then see the Disk."

"How do I find this guy . . . Erifani?"

"This is the difficult part." She paused. "You must use the Red Disk to find Erifani Tup. And you must find Erifani Tup in order to use the Red Disk. It is quite the conundrum, don't you think?"

Every computer chip in my skinny brain was trying to tell me I'd just gone insane.

"I . . . what . . . what?" I must've sounded like a complete idiot.

"Jimmy, your time is almost gone. I will tell you once more, and you must not forget. To find Erifani Tup, you must use the Red Disk. To use the Red Disk you must find Erifani Tup. You can do this, I know you can. The Dream Warden will then be revealed to you, and the Fourth Gift will be yours. Now, go."

"But—"

"Go. Come to me again, when it is all over. I will show you the Storm World, and you will never forget."

"But—"

"GO!"

Tingling prickles skittered all over my skin, which should have been a warning, but I was still lost trying to understand the Lady of the Storm's riddles. So I didn't notice the massive bolt of lightning until it was on top of us.

The world disintegrated into a million pieces of light and fire.

CHAPTER 57

To Bounce up a Hill

The blast of pure energy seemed to warp the fabric of reality, and its intense repercussions against the Shield knocked every ounce of breath from my lungs. I catapulted into the air with no sense of direction or understanding of what was happening. Tendrils of jagged electricity trailed behind me like ribbons on a kite, and before any part of my brain began to comprehend where I was going, I slammed into the side of a large pyramid.

Because of the great speed caused by the lightning, and the upward tilt of the pyramid, the Shield did not rebound me back toward the flat purple plain, but instead skipped me like a rock on a stream up the side of the pyramid. With no pain, only confusion, I bounded up the rain-drenched sides of the glowing edifice, until it merged with another one, and then another. With all the grace of a pinball, I bounced this way and that, ever upward, my momentum declining just slightly every time the protective bubble of the Shield hit purple stone.

Once I slowed to the point where I could think clearly, and since each bounce took just a little more time, I made an almost unsettling conclusion. The Lady of the Storm had driven the building-sized lightning at me with an extraordinary amount of calculation. She knew that my time was short, and understood the law of whatever physics governed this place to such a degree that the force of her conjuring was pushing me straight toward the gateway back into the Blackness.

One more bounce, and I settled with a perfect landing on the flight of stairs along the edge of the pyramid that held the iron rings, only thirty steps or so from the base of the crystal rod. Shell-shocked, I looked down at my watch.

Twenty minutes.

The flood of rain continued from the dark sky, cascading in sheets down the smooth walls and stairs, rushing over my feet. I gathered my wits and pounded up the stairs, hating that I had to be so careful not to slip. One more joy ride down the water slide would seal my fate—there would never be time to make it back to the Ripping in that case.

With ten steps left, I remembered the Shadow Ka. I looked over to the nearest peak. The Ka was gone. I looked at another. Gone. I looked all around, taking another step or two up the stairs. I could see no Ka anywhere.

Then I noticed a black mass of something behind me—hard to see through the water, but definitely there. It was writhing, and shifting, and gathering, forming a pointed wedge, and a shiver of horror went up my spine.

The Ka were forming a battering ram, made of their own bodies, to destroy the base of the iron rings. Although they could not see me, they were not stupid, and although my rare Gift had bought me precious time, the events down on the plain with the Lady had given me away.

My heart pounding, I turned toward the crystal beam and

looked up at the gateway that it supported. It was twenty feet above me. I looked back at the Shadow Ka. They were starting to move toward the gate.

I threw my thoughts into the power of the Ice, and it worked faster than ever before. A solid ladder of the cold and hard substance of my Gift formed in an instant, perhaps aided by so much water in the air, going from my feet to the top of the portal leading back into the Blackness. Without the slightest hint of hesitation, I jumped on it and began to climb.

Rung by slippery rung I flew up the ladder, reminded of the one I had built back at the Pointing Finger—although that had been my first try at the strange power, and hadn't looked nearly as professional.

Halfway up, I looked over my shoulder at the Ka. They were now coming full speed, flying as one, gathered into a tight knot with a deathly pointed end of blackness at its head. I swiveled my head back around and climbed the remaining distance to the topmost iron ring, and jumped into the gateway.

I was facing the coming onslaught of Ka, and they were on a straight course to destroy the crystal rod, shattering along with it my hopes of seeing anyone I loved ever again. They were almost there.

I knew it would take a few seconds, like always, but it was maddening.

Two seconds passed.

Three.

The Ka were getting closer and closer, screams now erupting from their writhing conglomerate in unison, deafening and shrill.

Four seconds passed. Five. *Come on,* I thought. *Come on, come on, come on!*

Six seconds. Nothing. Seven.

The point of the Ka's battering ram made contact with the crystal rod.

Eight seconds.

It sliced into the glass, penetrating it with a sound like colliding glaciers.

Nine seconds. I screamed it out loud this time: "COME ON!"

The iron rings tilted and began to fall, the sounds of shattered glass below deadened by the torrential rain. In sickened horror I thought it was truly over.

There was a flash of light, and the rain and terror ended.

My hands gripped the iron rings on the Blackness side of the portal, and I coaxed myself into breathing as I looked at the comforting surroundings of mist, stone, and inky waters—a disturbing thought in and of itself. I jumped out of the gateway and kicked myself for remembering far too late that I probably could've stopped the Ka with the Ice somehow. So I wasn't so good under pressure—big deal, it had all worked out.

My watch revealed that I had fifteen full minutes to get to the Ripping.

Piece of cake—too easy.

I stumbled across the jagged, torn up landing of the Storm World portal until I made it to the unblemished black marble of the pathway. Then I took off running with all the energy I could muster from within my exhausted skin-and-bones body.

Halfway there, I looked at my watch again.

Thirteen minutes.

By the time I reached the gaping hole leading to my sweet land of Earth, I still had eleven minutes. A swelling of pride and joy filled me as I remembered the Red Disk sitting in my backpack four inches from my heart. Having been set to a daunting task in an impossibly short period of time, I had done it with minutes to spare.

Of course, considering my luck, I should've known better than to think such things.

It was not over.

CHAPTER 58

Useless Gifts

I stepped through the Ripping and my breath was knocked out of me when I made the transition from moist, warm air to sub-zero frigidity. The glare of the sun against the endless snow of the North Pole snapped my eyes shut, and I put my hand over them until they could begin to adjust. My drenched clothes hardened into ice.

When I could manage a squint or two, I saw Hood to my right, shivering uncontrollably, the Bender Ring on the ground by his side.

"I did it, Hood!" I yelled, and walked over to him.

I expected a pat on the back or some other subtle hint from the wordless wonder, but instead he grabbed my arm and pointed frantically to the east. I followed his direction.

A lone Shadow Ka was flying straight toward us.

It was still a few seconds from reaching us, but I could see that the evolution of our enemy was close to complete. The skin was almost purely black now, and its arms and legs no longer resembled any aspect of humanity. Its massive wings flapped with a vengeance as it flew at us, and its familiar cry of death rocked the air.

"Why is it alone?" I asked.

Hood shrugged his shoulders, but then halted and pointed again.

It was not alone after all—it was just the leader. Behind it, a cloud of hundreds of other Ka followed in a tight pack. Their eruptive cries became audible now, as if by seeing them, we'd made them real.

"Well, whatever, let's get out of here," I said.

Hood made no argument. He bent over, grabbed the Bender Ring, and moved closer to me so we could travel back to my family.

But we had underestimated the speed of the flying Ka. In a sudden terror we saw that there wasn't enough time to even raise the Ring to where it needed to be. On instinct, I grabbed Hood's arm to protect him with my Shield.

The Ka swooped down, straight for me, screaming again and again. It reached out its shadowy talons, intent on grabbing me or ripping me in half. But how could it possibly be stupid enough to think it could get past the Shield? For good measure, I shot a ball of Ice right at its face when it got to within ten feet.

The Ice disintegrated inches before the Ka. I hurried another shot—the Ka now only five feet away. It didn't touch the beast, disappearing in a poof of mist.

"What—" was all I got out.

To my terrified surprise, the Ka's talons ignored the Shield and closed around my shirt and gripped me into its clutches. Hood, ignored, fell to the ground in confusion. Pulling me to its chest with a vicious squeeze, the Ka flew through the Ripping of the Black Curtain.

I was right back in the Blackness.

My Gifts had failed.

The next moments were a blur of movement, color, and fear. The brightness and snow evaporated into the darkness, and then the familiar images of the Blackness formed around us. The Ka was crushing my body, and it took every effort to keep breathing. After bursting through the opening of the Rip, the Ka banked hard to the left and flew out over the silvery water of the sea. It pulled to a stop twenty feet from the marble path and hovered in place with a rhythmic beating of its wings.

The hundreds of chasing Shadow Ka had also entered the otherworldly realm, and were swarming around us, gathering to devour me. The Ice. The Shield. What had happened? Why had they failed? An eating dread consumed me, and the thought of what kind of death was about to come my way was sickening and unbearable. A writhing cyclone of shadow spun around us. The lone Ka holding me was turning in place, scanning his brothers who surrounded us, communicating with its lightless eyes, readying for my final doom.

The Ka, now almost fully transformed from human to dragon-like beast, with barely any tattered human clothes remaining, swiveled its head down to look at me. Its eyes were the darkness of deep space, but there was an odd shift in them that made me suspect it had some feeling in its black heart. Shattered by the loss of my Gifts, I hung in its arms without struggling, too confused and scared to attempt an escape. The Ka's stare lingered, and then it screamed its furious roar. The pain of it pierced my ears, and I closed my eyes, knowing it was really going to end—after all the wasted efforts to save my own world.

The Ka threw me back toward the black path.

I flipped through the air and landed on the path with a slight surge from the Shield lessening its impact. The Shield. It had worked. What . . .

The Ka screamed one more time then dove into the sea, the water too heavy to make much of a splash. The mass of other Ka above it screeched as well and dove for the one who had just thrown me away.

It was at that moment that I understood.

CHAPTER 59

Swimming against Time

I jumped to my feet and screamed.

"NOOOOOOOO!"

I wanted to jump in, to go after him. It was Dad, it had to be Dad. Hanging on to his last chunk of humanity, he'd escaped with the intent to end his life—knowing that it was the only way to prevent himself from participating in the demonic plan of the Stompers. I knew from my earlier visits that there was something about the waters of the Blackness—that they were deadly to the Shadow Ka. Dad had done the only thing he felt was left to him.

That was why the Gifts had not worked. The inner workings of those special powers were something beyond comprehension—that they could know it was my dad, and not allow the Gifts to hurt him or hinder his good intent. The last half hour had once again awakened me to the incredible capacity of my almost ridiculous abilities.

The swarm of Ka diving after Dad pulled up just short of the water, having just missed him before he sank below the surface. They continued their shrieks, and hovered as one, flying to and fro above where Dad had fallen. They would not so much as test the water with their claws, fully aware of its effect on them. I stood and stared, my face empty and drawn, and then sunk to my knees as my heart began to tell me that Dad had just sacrificed his life.

I looked back and forth, straining to see through the chaos of the Ka for any sign of Dad resurfacing. I screamed for him, and the tears streamed down my face. Why, why did this have to happen to him? Why did they choose him out of all the people in the world?

I knew the answer, of course. It was my fault. They did it to get to me—to make me surrender. But Dad would not let them succeed, and this was his only way. My chest heaved with an unexpected sob, and I let it all out.

"DAD!" I yelled through the tears. "DAAAAAAAAD!"

I slumped, put my hands on the ground, and hung my head. With no real concern, I glanced at my stopwatch.

Five minutes.

Who cares? I asked myself.

Four minutes, fifty seconds.

Dad cared—enough to sacrifice his life.

Four minutes, forty seconds.

I must go, I thought, or his selflessness would be a waste. I had to get out with the Red Disk.

Four minutes, thirty seconds.

Pulling myself together, I got up and ran to the Ripping.

Just before I jumped through, I heard the wet bubbling of someone surfacing in the water, and I stopped dead. Daring to hope, I looked over.

Dad was there, treading in silver water, fully healed. Fully *healed.* There was no trace of the beast he had been seconds before.

"Jimmy!" he yelled, his voice wet with phlegm, barely audible over the sounds of the Ka screaming above him. "Jimmy! The water saved me somehow!"

My jaw was probably hanging around my toes, and my heart had stopped completely.

"I'm coming, son!" He pushed forward his hands and began the swim back.

The Ka were not going to let him live. It was so unfair. It was such a cruel trick. Brought back from the dead in the last instant, beyond all reason or hope—all for naught. His former comrades, the ones he refused to join, were coming in for the kill.

I looked down at the watch with dread. Three minutes. I sprung into action.

I ran back the forty or fifty feet I had traveled, closer to the point to which Dad was swimming. As I ran, I called upon the Ice with a flurry of concentration. Bullets of Ice ripped through the air, swarming in from all directions, exploding Ka by Ka away from my Dad. It took every ounce of my effort, every detectable piece of will within me to keep them away.

For every one I hit, three more dove for Dad. Some made contact before I blew them off with the Ice. His shoulders were getting bloody from the scratches. I continued my assault, yelling out loud, still running. Balls of Ice shot through the air with ferocity, blasting the Ka away from Dad and into a watery death. The water was not healing them like it had my dad, but I didn't have time to figure it out. The wailing sound of dying Ka began to drown out the screams of the ones still vying to destroy my dad.

I came to a stop, now in a direct line to Dad's swimming path. His arms were weary, his face droopy with exhaustion. I couldn't spare the energy to call to him, to encourage him. It took everything I had to keep the Ka away, obliterating them with my Gift of Ice.

I could *feel* the seconds ticking away as I continued my barrage of frozen warfare. The point where we would never make it was fast approaching.

The Ka did not quit—oblivious to fear, oblivious to death. They attacked in pairs now, trying anything to overcome my abilities. I held firm, and Dad swam with every last bit of effort he could find within his weakened body. He was only a few body lengths away.

A Ka got through, ripping a six-inch gash across Dad's back. I blew the creature away, its scream dying out with a gurgling gasp as it sank into the sea. Another Ka ripped some hair from Dad's head before I dealt with it. It was growing more difficult—they would not be stopped.

Closer he came. Only a few feet. I just needed to touch his hand and it would all be over. I considered jumping in, but couldn't take the risk. He was almost to me—only a couple of feet from my outstretched hand. The gash on his shoulder had already healed—the magic of the Blackness that I had almost forgotten about.

The remaining Ka, sensing their last opportunity, gathered into one, just like I'd seen at the Storm World gateway, and swooped in with a vengeance. I gave up on the Ice and grabbed for Dad's hand. His fingers clasped into mine just as the mass of Ka exploded into us. Knowing his hands were wet, I took extra care as I gripped Dad's hand with every bit of strength I owned.

The Shield expanded, and the diving Ka slammed into its invisible protection. A quick series of thumps announced their collision with it, and they rebounded away in all directions, yelling their piercing calls of furious rage. Most fell into the water, the few that remained giving up and flying away, defeated, back through the Ripping fifty feet away.

Dad was exhausted. I grabbed his arms and pulled, pulling him out of the water and onto the marble path with almost no help. He was almost naked, and his skin was pale and sickly.

"Son, I'm sorry I grabbed you . . . sorry I put you in danger . . . I wasn't thinking . . ." were the only things he had enough energy to say.

"Dad, we don't have enough time—come on!"

Calling upon every remaining spurt of adrenaline within me, I pulled Dad's arm up and around my neck, and screamed out loud with effort as I helped him to a standing position.

"Try to walk, Dad—we're almost there, and then you can rest!"

I felt him put weight onto his legs and feet, as much as he could, and we began the long walk back to the Ripping. My right arm was wrapped around Dad's back, and my left arm pushed on his chest to help him balance as we walked. I looked at the watch on my left wrist, right below my face.

Twenty seconds.

Like two drunken men in a three-legged race, we hurried as fast as we could down the path. My body hurt with the effort of supporting Dad, and begged me to give up.

Fifteen seconds.

Step by lumbering step we shuffled down the path, getting closer with each one.

Ten seconds.

Dad stumbled, the exhaustion too much. We fell to the ground with a thump, and I looked up in panic. The Ripping was still twenty feet away. There was just no way—it was impossible. We weren't going to make it! I looked down.

Five seconds.

Four.

Three.

Two.

One.

The sound of static electricity filled the air, and the Ripping began to close.

CHAPTER 60

The World Bends

I don't know if there was a measurable amount of time in which my brain processed several thoughts, but in the nanoseconds it took for the Rip to seal shut, I considered my options. Maybe I could shoot the Ice and somehow keep the Rip open for just a little longer. Maybe I could shoot Dad through it with a beam of the cold Second Gift, and hope it didn't cut him in half. Or, we could stay, and take our chances in the Blackness. But none of these were truly options—the risks were too high, the implications too dreadful. There was, really, only one choice.

I called upon the Anything for the second time.

With little time to be creative, I flung out the first coherent thought I could formulate. With every ounce of will inside of my heart, I ordered the Anything to reunite my family no matter what it took. To make it a solid invoking of the Gift, leaving no room for doubt, I imagined it happening in the first specific location that popped in my head.

The stable where we had left the horses.

In perhaps the oddest use of my Gifts thus far, I called upon the Anything to take us all to Baka.

Baka the horse.

It would be difficult for someone of my admittedly great but still limited brain to formulate the right words to describe what then happened. The very substance of time seemed to shift, and the world around me bent horribly. I could not move my head, but somehow I was aware of everything that happened around me, and even the occurrences of things thousands of miles away. Time and distance lost all meaning, and I could see everything.

The closing of the Curtain stopped in its tracks and bubbled outward to provide enough room. Dad was beside me one instant, and then a flash of color—a streak of almost imperceptible movement—and he was gone, slicing through the air and out of the Blackness. A millisecond later, I exploded out of the Blackness as well, through the Ripping, and tore through the air at a blistering pace.

But we were not flying. At least I felt no sense of passing air, I hit no ducks on the way, had no time to wave at passersby. I felt nothing—no sense of movement at all, no awareness of my surroundings on the way. Everything was a blur of chaos. We were not traveling—we were simply *changing locations*.

Every color in the spectrum, every creature on Earth, every climate, every landscape, millions of people passed my vision in brief flashes, like someone running past an open window, seen through the corner of the eye. The world spun below us, as if some alien giant was twirling it on a green, warty finger. Instead of experiencing feelings of motion, it was like Japan was coming to me.

Mom and Rusty, in similar fashion miles away, exploded out of a wayside motel in Japan, a gaping hole in the walls of the place temporarily obliterated to allow them passage, and then reforming as if it had never happened. Our minds and emotions were traumatized by the sudden weirdness of it all.

I will never know what forces of nature or physics or magic were called upon to meet the demands of my new and formidable Gift. I will never know if it took minutes or hours. But my last memory of the journey was seeing the roof of the horse stable melt away, and then standing there, next to Dad, Mom, Rusty, and a dirty, hungry horse named Baka.

I looked up and the roof was whole again, seemingly never touched.

For a second, a wall of confusion kept any of us from moving. But then it melted away, and we all embraced. Dad, smelling like garbage and pasted with inky slime, was overcome with emotion, and I thought for sure he was going to puncture one of my lungs with his vice-like hug. He acted like if he ever let go, we might just vanish once and for all, with no more second chances.

We were together again. Confused as heck, but together again.

Somewhere in the back of my mind I had the passing thought that the Anything could only be used two more times.

But I didn't care.

CHAPTER 61

Odd Visitor

Later that night, we sat in a hotel room watching TV, witnessing the world fall into more chaos. The Shadow Ka were increasing their area of terror, expanding now to the smaller cities and rural neighborhoods. The small port town we huddled in seemed okay still, although the people refused to venture out from their homes. The days were growing darker as the frightful shadow of the skies increased. The nights were even worse—moonless and empty. And I missed Rayna and Miyoko terribly.

When we returned to the hotel after our reunion, we'd found Joseph and Hood waiting for us, fretful and impatient. When the Shadow Ka version of my dad grabbed and pulled me into the Blackness, Hood had fallen to the wayside, forgotten in the confusion as the remnants of the chasing pack of Ka screamed their fury and left the area in a blizzard of black wings. Apparently they were not willing to get stuck in the Blackness again after waiting so long for the blocking I had invoked to finally end.

In the blistering instant when Dad and I had torn through

the Black Curtain at the last moment, Hood had seen a blur of color, and then the Ripping had closed. With a heavy feeling of regret that we had not made it, he'd used the Bender Ring to return to the hotel where Joseph, Mom, and Rusty were staying, only to find Joseph as confused as he was.

But now we sat together again, our eyes glued to the increasing doom on the television. Only a couple of national news channels remained on the air—the rest having succumbed to the wave of coma-inducing Shadow Ka. The world was on the brink of some horrible thing that we did not fully understand.

We had no idea what had happened to the agents of the Secret Service, but we'd seen no sign of them, and they had never come after the rest of my family. Luckily, Joseph had gotten the new rooms under his name, and it looked like he wasn't yet important enough to be hunted by the United States government.

"My gosh," Mom said, "what's going to happen now?"

"The whole world is in complete chaos!" Joseph said. "Jimmy, what's next?"

"I don't know," was my very insufficient reply. "I have no idea. Somehow we have to figure out a few things."

I told them everything I could remember, and showed them the Red Disk. About the cyclic riddle of how only Erifani Tup could show how to use the Disk, but you needed the Disk to find him. About how the Disk would then reveal the Dream Warden, and how he or she or it would then reveal the Fourth Gift.

The final Gift. Farmer had said it would be far more powerful than the Anything, which seemed so impossible. But I knew he was telling the truth.

Dad also told us his story of escape during that long, sleepless night.

Lost in a world of madness inside his own brain, which he refused to discuss any further, he'd slowly but surely felt his transformation into one of the Ka. Sometime after his wings had finally formed, he began to wake from the darkness, ready to serve his new masters.

But deep within, he held onto some semblance of himself, refusing to let the evil override him completely. Still on the fancy airplane where we'd last seen him, with the kind-of-human Raspy, they'd taken off to the skies, the old monster saying he wasn't taking any chances on recovering the Red Disk, and that they were going to retrieve it when we came back into the world up at the North Pole. Circling overhead, with an army of Shadow Ka surrounding them for support, they had waited. Hood had seen this but could do nothing.

When Dad overheard Raspy and some other person discussing how the waters of the Blackness destroyed the Shadow Ka, he knew it was his only chance to prevent himself from succumbing fully one day, and serving the Stompers.

So he'd reached down inside of himself and pulled everything good to the forefront, and in a furious burst of energy and will, he'd escaped, bursting through the airplane door, almost causing the thing to crash. He flew away with an army of Shadow Ka behind him. When he saw me standing there by the Ripping, his instincts took over and he grabbed my shirt to protect me from the Ka chasing him from behind, even though I would've been just fine because of the Gifts.

The rest I had witnessed first hand. Why he survived while the other Ka that fell in the water did not, remained a mystery. But we figured it had something to do with the good that still held tight inside my dad, despite his turning into a Shadow Ka. Perhaps the silvery sea cleans away all that is evil, and the rest of the Ka had nothing left after the process. We didn't know the answer for sure, and right then we didn't care.

After his story, there wasn't much talk. The next day would bring more troubles, more pain, more sorrow, more adventures, more confusion, more of everything that had come to define my life. But for the rest of that night, we tried our best to put it all aside, eat some decent food, and pretend like all was well. We were still on a high of having been reunited, but it was impossible to ignore what lay ahead.

Approaching midnight, we were almost ready to give up our forced happiness. Having decided to be extra safe and all sleep in the same room, no matter how crowded, we allowed ourselves to get some sleep.

That was when we heard the knock on the door.

When Joseph opened it, and we saw the person standing there, all symptoms of weariness evaporated like a rattlesnake teardrop in a mid-summer desert.

It was Tanaka.

But that wasn't the most shocking part.

It was what he held in his hands.

Epilogue

The next morning, I was in a stable, talking to a horse.

"Baka, old buddy," I said, not in the least bit embarrassed to be speaking to my favorite animal in the world. "I have to admit, I'm scared to death. To make matters worse, I can't even remember the last time I wore a Braves hat."

I brushed his coat, knowing that horses liked that sort of thing. It was strange that I felt so bonded to the big brown fella, but then again, when you'd been to the brink of death and back with someone—be it human or horse—you sort of felt a connection.

"You wouldn't believe who came trouncing into our hotel last night."

I paused, as if Baka might actually take a stab at guessing.

"Time's up. It was Tanaka. We'd thought for sure he was fish food, but he showed up last night like nothing had ever happened. Wouldn't even tell us much, just kept whining that 'he so tired, gathered all of them' and some other nonsense."

Baka sneezed, or coughed, or whatever it is when a horse

makes that loud, lip-vibrating noise that spews stinky horse phlegm everywhere.

"I know, weird, huh? None of us have a clue what he was talking about, and he fell asleep before we could get one more word out of him. But that wasn't the weirdest thing."

Again, I gave Baka a chance to read my mind, but he went for some yummy oats instead.

"You don't even care, do you?" I patted him on the head, and told him that I'd come to see him again later.

As I walked to the stable doors, I paused, and looked back.

"You're dying to know, aren't you?" I asked the four-legged creature.

He let out a slight snicker, and nodded his head. Honest to goodness, the horse nodded his head.

"He had a big wire cage with him," I said. "It was completely full of . . . something, and we still have no idea why."

Baka's eyes bore into mine, anxious for either the next part of the story, or some more oats, I'll never know. But I told him anyway.

"The cage was full of butterflies."

❦

As I left Baka behind, and headed off in search of breakfast with my family, my heart was heavy with a sense of approaching duty and danger.

Deep inside of me, I felt something within my blood and bones, although I don't think my mind fully comprehended the feeling I was having. But somehow, I knew.

It was all about to come to a head, the day of reckoning,

the day things would be decided with either dreaded finality or perpetual hope.

And I would be ready.

The battle of all time and substance was about to begin.

To be concluded in . . .

Book Four of the
Jimmy Fincher Saga,
War of the Black Curtain

About the Author

James Dashner was born and raised in Georgia. Although he currently resides in Utah, he will always be a southerner at heart.

After high school, James attended Brigham Young University, where he went on to receive a master's degree in accounting. He also took a couple of years off and served a mission in Japan. Since graduation, he has received his CPA, worked for a major audit firm, and now works as a financial analyst.

He is married and has three children.

For more information on James and The Jimmy Fincher Saga, visit www.jamesdashner.com or email him at author@ jamesdashner.com.

About the Illustrator

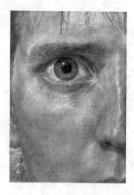

Michael Phipps grew up spending hours with friends drawing, imagining other worlds, making odd recordings, and building marble chutes and forts. He always knew he would be an artist as an adult, and he graduated with a bachelor of fine arts degree in illustration from the University of Utah. He loves to spend time with his family and friends, be outdoors, and listen to strange music. His art can be viewed at www.michael-phipps.net. E-mail him at art@michaelphipps.net.